WOLF SCENT

ISABEL DARE

Copyright © 2013 Isabel Dare

All rights reserved.

ISBN: 1494432374
ISBN-13: 978-1494432379

It was a gorgeous fall day, crisp and clear, and the scent of woodsmoke and pine hung in the air. It was three days before the next full moon, and Kirk was already beginning to feel that rising tide of power tugging at his blood.

His skin itched, and his clothes felt uncomfortable. His beard grew back so fast that there was no point in shaving, because he'd just end up with a face full of bristles by the end of the day.

As he let the axe swing into the wood with a resounding *thwock,* he knew that his strength was growing, too. He had already chopped enough wood for a week, and he still didn't feel tired.

It helped, Kirk thought for the thousandth time, that he lived in the mountains and didn't have to talk to anyone on days like these. It didn't help *enough* —nothing helped against the sickness in his blood, the taint that turned him into a beast three nights a month —but it was a comfort. Kirk loved Sevenacres, the small town in the valley below; it was a haven of comfort and familiarity. He just couldn't go there.

Not today, not until the moon had loosened its hold on him. If he went into town now, he would lose whatever good will he had managed to gather there, by growling at people and breaking things. It was easy to break things when his hands felt like they already had claws, just waiting to leap out from beneath his nails.

And the scents—oh no, he couldn't deal with the scents of civilization when it was too close to full moon. Gasoline, dogs, perfume, restaurant food, cigarette smoke: even when they didn't smell horrible, the scents became so incredibly distinct and vivid that he could lose himself in them, forget where he was and what he was doing.

That was a good way to get run over. And while he would probably survive almost any accident, he *really* didn't want to wake up in a hospital just before the change.

Kirk stacked up the wood under the overhanging eaves of his cabin and tied a tarp over the woodpile.

Then he just stood there for a moment, feeling the restless, rising urge of his blood and wondering what to do with himself. He worked as a handyman, doing odd jobs and chores for people in the town below and in the other cabins, but he always took care not to take on any assignment that would require him to work on days like these.

He could go hunting…but it might stir up his blood lust to a feverish height, and he didn't want to come home with a torn-apart deer he didn't even remember killing.

Sighing, Kirk decided to just go for a long, punishing run. It wouldn't help the restless wolf in him, but it might at least tire him out enough to sleep well tonight.

He ran upstairs, stripped off his flannel shirt and jeans, and quickly changed into an old black track suit and his running shoes.

Then he was off, his hair streaming behind him in the crisp wind, his long legs setting a brisk pace.

Kirk chose a trail he knew so well that he could

have run it blindfolded. It wound up and up the mountain in long serpentine coils, all the way up to Deering Pass and past the lookout point at Wolfshead Rock.

The trail was an old mule-trail from the logging days, and it wasn't used much now; it was not an official walking trail and there were no signs or blazes to guide a tourist. That was a bonus, as far as Kirk was concerned. He didn't want to risk meeting anyone he knew.

Kirk ran and ran, enjoying the burn of cool mountain air in his lungs and the springy leaf mold under his feet. It was so much better than running on asphalt. The ground almost seemed to be helping him, giving him just a bit of added lift.

The animal scents were so clear up here, too. Fox, rabbit, a faint hint of bear, probably a black bear foraging for nuts and berries. And there, a strong scent of deer, musky and familiar. An older stag, rubbing his antlers against a tree.

This time of the month, Kirk could distinguish between male and female deer, young and old, sick and healthy.

None of those things smelled bad, not to his

wolf nose. Just *interesting*.

Kirk often tried to remember what it was like to be a normal human being, to smell only what humans could smell, but even on new moon days, when his beast self was weakest, his senses were still so much sharper than a human's. Scent was a three-dimensional, overwhelming sensation, richer than color, sometimes even more intense than touch.

Old scents painted a time-lapse portrait of what had happened somewhere, up to several days ago, vivid enough that he could see it in his mind's eye.

New scents gave a vivid picture of everything a person or animal had eaten, drunk, and touched.

And there was still more to it than that… especially for human scents. A man's or woman's scent had components that were more subtle, more difficult to distinguish, and strongly tied to their personality. Over time, Kirk had learned to tell if someone was scared, pleased, angry, lying, turned on, or repulsed from their scent alone, and he tended to judge character by scent as well. His nose seldom steered him wrong.

On and on he ran, moving higher up the mountain, where pine cones crunched under his feet and the air was crisp and cool. The sun was setting, and it would be dark in an hour. Not that that would pose a problem to Kirk. He could see better in the dark, and he could probably navigate home by scent alone. But the night, the waxing moon, would bring his wolf out even stronger, and he preferred to be indoors by then.

He paused for a moment by a small stream that ran across the path. It welled straight from the rock, the water springing forth crystal clear and cold from some hidden underground source.

Kirk cupped his hand under the trickle and drank.

Ahh, the taste of pure spring water. There was another spring-fed stream closer to the cabin, where Kirk's father had once built a cool house, and every week Kirk went back and forth, filling big jugs to stock up the cabin's drinking water. It was primitive to some, maybe, but it tasted better than the water from the municipal pipes.

As he stood there by the stream, catching his breath, feeling the pleasant burn in his muscles, he suddenly caught a new scent. An amazing, complex scent he had never encountered before. It overwhelmed him, dizzying him with its promise.

Human, but uniquely enticing—like discovering an entirely new species.

Instinctively, he let his head fall back, swiveling to catch the scent on the wind.

There. He had the direction now.

Kirk started running.

The scent was getting stronger now with every step, and he breathed in full gasps, drawing it deeper into his lungs.

It smelled better than any food he had ever eaten, any animal he had ever hunted, any man he had ever had sex with, on those few nights when he succumbed to the urges of pent-up desire.

Deep and complex, a whole orchestra of scent, with overtones of sunlight on freshly rained-on grass and undertones of a peppery heat that made him want to howl.

Kirk kept running, following the scent as though his life depended on it. It felt like it did. It felt like it would kill him to lose this wonder.

Pure instinct ruled him—he couldn't stop, couldn't let the thinking, human part of him take over.

Not now.

And now that he was getting closer, he could smell other things. Pain, fear, and blood. They didn't belong to the wondrous scent, but they were part of it, twisted around it, threatening it. Marring its beauty.

He crashed through thick thorn bushes, barely noticing the scratches, and came to an abrupt halt in a small clearing under a large and spreading oak tree.

In front of him, kneeling, was the source of his scent.

A young man with dirty blond hair, his face obscured as he curled in upon himself, both hands wrapping around his outstretched left leg. Vicious metal teeth bit deep into his calf, and Kirk could see blood all over his leg and hands. His breath came fast and high, and he was clearly in agony.

His leg was caught in a huge steel trap. A very old bear trap, by the looks of it, that had been buried here long ago when the mountain wasn't a nature reserve and bear trapping was still legal.

Kirk had to get the trap off him, but without hurting him further. That was going to be tricky.

This close, the scent of the young man's pain

was overwhelming everything else. It was hard to remember how to speak, how to be human. Kirk wanted to sniff at the young man, put his ears forward and his tail up, telling him wordlessly that he was a friend.

Kirk took a cautious step closer, not wanting to startle him.

The young man looked up, and his eyes widened.

"Oh god," he said faintly. Then, stronger, "Am I trespassing? I'm sorry. I got lost—"

Kirk stared at him, baffled. "What?" he said.

"Please don't shoot me," the young man said, his voice thready. Maybe he was in shock.

Kirk shook his head. "Don't worry."

What was he talking about? Kirk wasn't armed.

Kirk knelt by his side, thinking that maybe towering over him wasn't going to help. Plus, this way he could get a better look at his leg.

The young man shrank back, looking terrified, his eyes wide and hunted.

Suddenly Kirk realized what he must look like. Big and burly, dressed in uncompromising black, his hair a tangle, his beard rough and unkempt. Like some kind of wild man of the mountain, maybe. Some crazy hermit who shot strangers on sight.

And the young man was dressed like a hiker, not a local—fancy outdoor jacket, big boots, huge rucksack lying by his head. Probably a stranger to these mountains.

"Don't worry," Kirk said again, trying to make his voice sound gentle. It didn't come naturally, especially not today, but he tried. "I want to help. What's your name?"

"Leo," the young man said. "I don't think…"

He paused, swallowing hard, and his face lost a little more color. The scent of pain grew stronger. "I don't think this thing comes off," he said in a thin voice. "I tried. I tried for hours."

Kirk nodded reassuringly. "Good," he said.

Leo stared at him with those wide eyes. "Good?"

"Means it didn't hit your femoral artery," Kirk explained. "That would kill you in minutes."

"That's very reassuring," Leo said slowly.

Kirk thought he could see a hint of a smile on his white, pain-drawn face; battlefield humor, masking his agony.

Then the young man's face sobered, and his voice stuttered when he said, "Just, you can't—take it off me. It's so strong. Couldn't move it. Need to—get help."

Kirk moved closer until he was kneeling over Leo, filling his field of vision.

"Listen," he said. "Leo."

Kirk could see Leo's white, drawn face relax slightly at the sound of his name. It was something Kirk remembered from his old army training: using someone's first name helped to keep them calm during a traumatic situation.

"I'm going to open the trap," Kirk said, slowly, waiting to see if Leo was going to protest again that he couldn't do it. He needed Leo with him on this.

Leo stared up at him, his breath hitching, and nodded slowly. "Okay."

"I'm going to need both hands to keep it

open," Kirk went on, watching him closely to see if he was following. "It's probably going to feel good for a moment as the pressure goes away. Then it's going to hurt like hell when the air hits those holes in your leg."

Leo nodded, his expression dubious. Probably he was thinking, *How can this possibly hurt worse?*

"When I say 'go'," Kirk told him, "I need you to move backwards. Use your elbows to scoot back, then slide your leg out of the trap. You don't need to move fast. Just keep going until your leg is completely clear. Got that?"

"When you say 'go', I move back," Leo repeated, his voice thready but clear. "Got it."

"Okay," Kirk said, hoping Leo wasn't faking this level of clarity. He knew what it was like to be in a world of shock and pain. It was damn hard to follow instructions.

Watching Leo's eyes to make sure he stayed conscious, Kirk took a deep breath and began to feel for the edge of the trap.

The teeth bit deep, past shredded jeans and into Leo's flesh.

Kirk had to dig around in the earth to get a

good grip on the old springs at the side of the trap.

He could hear Leo's breath, thin and ragged from the pain. His scent swirled around Kirk, overlaid with the dark sour smells of fear and pain and the coppery tang of blood, but underneath it all was still that warm, grassy brightness that was so damnably attractive.

"Take a deep breath," Kirk told him, and began to depress the springs. They were very old, very strong, and rusty.

With traps of this size and power, the traditional method to open them took two men, both standing on top of each spring. Kirk's body weight wasn't going to be enough. This needed his wolf strength.

For the first time since he'd been turned into a monster, Kirk felt a spark of gratitude for the wolf blood inside him. The blood that made him stronger than any man, with better reflexes.

It had only been a source of grief to him before, but now he could use it to help someone.

To help Leo.

"Oh," Leo said faintly when the teeth began to

move apart. His blue eyes were very wide and shocky. "How are you—how can—"

Kirk felt the huge, tremendously strong springs of the trap fighting against him.

The teeth didn't want to let go. The trap was built for one purpose: to catch and to kill a full-grown bear. Or a man.

Not today, he thought with a fierce anger that surprised him. *Not him.*

Fresh blood welled up as the jaws of the trap slowly creaked open.

Kirk could tell the instant when the edged teeth drew clear of Leo's leg. Leo inhaled harshly, then gave a single, wailing cry that hurt Kirk's ears.

After that he was silent, except for breathless sobs of pain. Just as Kirk had told him, fresh air hitting the open wounds was agony.

Kirk felt like a torturer, even though he knew he was saving the other man's life.

The jaws of the trap slid open, wider, wider still, with the springs protesting all the way.

Now Kirk was leaning on his hands, right

above the open jaws of the trap.

"Go," he said loudly and distinctly. "Slide back, get your leg out."

Leo blinked dazedly, and for a moment Kirk despaired. If Leo fainted, things were about to get much more difficult.

But then Leo began to move. He braced himself on his elbows, awkwardly hitching himself back.

"Good," Kirk told him, relieved. "Keep going."

Slowly, Leo inched backward, hissing when his wounded leg dragged over the ground. He used his right leg to push himself away from the trap, almost kicking Kirk in the face.

Now he was just far away enough that only his left foot was still inside the open trap.

"Keep going," Kirk said urgently. He could tell that Leo was on the verge of losing consciousness. "Leo! Just once more. Push back. *Move.*"

To his own ears, his voice sounded as unpleasant, harsh and demanding as his old drill sergeant's, but it worked.

With a desperate gasping effort, Leo pushed himself back.

His leg slid free.

With a sigh of relief, Kirk slowly, slowly edged back himself, careful of the immense power of the trap. He didn't want the thing to snap his nose off.

He let the pressure of his hands ease off, slowly releasing the springs. As soon as he snatched his hands away, the trap snapped shut again with a nasty metallic *thunk*, biting the empty air.

Leo watched him, pale and trembling with shock.

Kirk shook himself for a moment, getting rid of the tension in his shoulders, the fierce burn in his arms, and then slid over to Leo's position.

"Well done," Kirk told him, making an effort to gentle his voice again. "Now let's see your leg."

"I'm going to pass out," Leo told him firmly.

"Okay," Kirk said, a corner of his mouth quirking upward. "You don't need to be conscious for this part."

Leo nodded faintly, and then his eyes closed

and he dropped to one side, limp as a leaf.

Kirk bent over him, taking a sniff of his scent almost without realizing he was doing it. The taint of pain and blood was still strong, but the sour tang of fear had faded. Good.

Carefully, Kirk uncovered the wounded leg, brushing leaves away from Leo's torn jeans. There were several deep holes, bleeding sluggishly, and a lot of tears and bruises. No broken bones, as far as his hands could tell.

He would have to get Leo to a doctor, make sure there were no hairline fractures, and check if a tetanus shot was needed. But for the immediate future, Leo's wounds required bandaging, disinfectant and painkillers.

Luckily, Kirk was…unusually well supplied in that area. He had to be.Even in wolf form, he could be hurt.

Worse than that—he could hurt others. And there were only three days left before the wolf would take over.

Leo woke up alone.

For long moments, he just stared at the wooden beams above his head, trying to get a grip on reality. His dreams had been wild and exhausting, more like nightmares. Something about a forest and a monster…

Then he tried to sit up, and the pain hit.

Leo bit back a cry of agony and fell back into the pillows. What on earth—his leg was on *fire*, what the hell had he been doing—

Memory came crashing back.

Hiking. He'd gone hiking. Lost his way just as night was falling, and then that horrible trap had closed on his leg.

What a stupid way to die.

Except that he clearly wasn't dead, and this was neither heaven nor a hospital.

Where *was* he?

Leo blinked up at the ceiling, trying to arrange his thoughts. His brain felt fuzzy, as though he was recovering from a very drunk evening.

That man. Was he part of his dreams, or had that really happened? Had some six-foot hairy mountain man appeared out of nowhere to save him?

But in his fuzzy memories, the man had wrenched the bear trap open with his bare hands. That couldn't be right. Nobody was *that* strong.

And yet Leo thought he could remember being carried in the man's arms as he loped away down the path.

No rescue helicopters, no ambulances.

Just one man. If he *was* a man.

Leo laughed suddenly, imagining the tabloid headlines. *I Was Rescued By Bigfoot. The Sasquatch Who Saved Me.*

Then he winced as the laugh made his belly muscles cramp. Everything hurt.

Tilting his head, he tried to get a better view of the room he was in.

Yeah, definitely not a hospital. He was lying in someone's bedroom, a small comfortable room with white-painted wooden walls, an old rag rug on the floor, and not much furniture except the bed he was lying in. A colorful quilt covered the bottom part of the bed, and there was a picture on one wall. An oil painting, in a frame that might once have been gilt, but was now mostly black.

Leo squinted, trying to make out what was in the painting. It needed cleaning, and there was only a faint hint of glowing color underneath layers of discolored varnish and grime. His hands fairly itched to work on it.

It seemed to be a medieval scene of some sort, with knights on stylized horses and a lady sitting under an embroidered canopy. He wondered if it was the original work or a later copy.

His neck started to hurt, and Leo sighed and lay back, letting his gaze wander over the wooden beams above his head. Moving hurt too much, and he felt sleep weigh down his eyes again.

The important thing was that he was still alive.

Questions could wait, he told himself as he drifted back into sleep. Answers could wait.

Whatever had happened, someone had found him. Someone had rescued him, when he was trapped and alone and in excruciating pain.

And if that wasn't a miracle, it was the closest thing to it that Leo had ever known.

The door creaked when Kirk opened it, and for a second Kirk was annoyed that he hadn't thought to oil the hinges. Then he had to laugh at himself. *What, so you could steal into his room without him noticing? Yeah, great idea. That would definitely put your guest at ease.*

Leo was just waking up. He looked bleary, and his blond hair stood up around his head like a fuzzy crown; Kirk's hands itched to reach out and ruffle it even further.

"Ah…hi," Leo said, his voice a croak.

His eyes were growing wide as he looked at Kirk, and Kirk had no idea why.

Kirk had done his best to clean up a little—he'd even shaved, although his chin was beginning to prickle with emerging bristles already. And his current outfit of flannel shirt and blue jeans had to look less sombre than the all-black running gear, surely.

"Hi," Kirk said. His voice sounded strange to his own ears, and he cleared his throat.

It felt awkward, filling up the doorway like this. Bending his head to avoid the low door jamb, he stepped into the room.

"How are you feeling?" he asked. "Do you need more painkillers?"

Leo stared at him, then slowly said, "Not right now. I'd...I'd like to be awake for a while."

Now that he was this close, Kirk had to work hard to keep himself from inhaling loudly and noticeably. The other man's scent was subdued now, overlaid with the bitter haze of medicine, but it was still incredibly alluring. There was nothing artificial about it; no perfume or aftershave could ever hope to match such a pure natural scent, though he knew that a normal human being would not even notice it.

"I want to examine your leg," Kirk said. "Check for infection."

He knew it was too abrupt, that his voice sounded more like a growl, but he couldn't help himself. He had to regain some measure of control, even at the cost of civility.

"Okay," Leo said, but the set of his mouth was wary. "Are you a doctor?"

"No," Kirk admitted. He ran a hand through his hair. "I called Dr Ogilvy. It'll be some time before she gets here. She's got a difficult delivery on her hands."

There, that was better. He could see the tight set of Leo's shoulders easing as he spoke.

"So, my memories of what happened are pretty hazy," Leo said. "But…you got me out of the trap, right? That was you?"

Kirk nodded.

"And you carried me down the mountain?"

Kirk shrugged, but Leo stared at him with those big blue eyes until he felt compelled to add, "No big deal. You're not that heavy."

Leo gave a faint snort. "Well, it's a big deal to *me*." He paused, looking away. "You probably think I'm an idiot. A stupid tourist who gets lost and then steps into a bear trap."

"It happens," Kirk said with another shrug. "You were lucky."

Leo's shoulders slumped, and he sighed. "Right.""So…where am I?" He plucked at the sheets, still avoiding Kirk's eyes. "I'm guessing this is your house?"

Kirk nodded. "Cabin. Yes."

He took another step, bringing him up to the edge of the bed. He had to go through with this, as awkward as the situation was; he couldn't risk Leo's health to save his modesty.

"Let's see your leg."

Awkwardly, Leo unfolded the blankets, baring his legs to Kirk's view. He wore a hiking t-shirt and plain black boxers; Kirk had stowed his other clothes in a closet for now, along with his giant backpack.

It was an effort to keep himself from staring at Leo's thighs, or the tempting shadows between them. He had to focus. He had to make sure Leo was healing properly.

Moving slowly and carefully, Kirk removed the bandage from around Leo's hurt leg and looked at the wounds. Most of his leg was mottled black and purple with bruises, but the holes themselves were already closing up. Nasty-looking, but not infected, as far as he could tell; there was no swelling, no smell, no redness. No signs of danger.

Leo looked down at his leg too, then away, swallowing. "That looks awful."

Kirk nodded. "Would've looked worse if you'd lost the leg."

Leo shook his head. "Anyone ever tell you that your bedside manner is…a little disconcerting?"

"That's why I'm not a doctor," Kirk said, dry as dust.

Leo laughed at that, and Kirk felt an unaccustomed warmth settle beneath his breastbone. It wasn't often that he could make people laugh.

He unrolled some fresh bandages and wrapped Leo's leg again, trying to be gentle. Leo bit his lip, and Kirk knew it had to be hurting him now that the painkillers were wearing off, but he didn't make a sound.

"Doc'll be here in a couple hours," Kirk said. "Get some sleep."

He put a strip of painkillers and a glass of water on Leo's bedside table. "If things get bad, take one of these. Two at most."

Leo nodded. "Thanks."

Then, just as Kirk turned to leave, Leo said softly, "What's your name?"

Kirk paused and looked back over his shoulder. "Kirk Anderson."

"Thanks, Kirk," Leo said. He was smiling a little, his rosy mouth curving in a way that Kirk tried not to notice.

Kirk closed the door behind him, and then paused to knock his head into the wooden cabin wall with a gentle thump.

He was in *so* much trouble.

Dr Ogilvy was a brisk woman of about sixty, with steel-gray curls cropped close to her head. She examined Leo's leg just like Kirk had, though her hands were cooler and Leo didn't find himself suppressing shivers when she touched him.

"Good job," she said, patting Leo's unharmed leg. "I've seen bear trap wounds before, and they were much worse than yours."

Leo's mouth quirked. "Now you're just making me feel like a crybaby."

Dr Ogilvy gave a bark of laughter. "Well, I've just delivered one of those, and I can tell the difference."

She re-wrapped his leg and gave him instructions about the painkillers he could take. Then, after an embarrassing but necessary episode with a bedpan, Leo thought she was about to leave, but she sat down on the bed again and said, "So how's he been treating you?"

"You mean Kirk," Leo said.

Dr Ogilvy nodded. Her eyes were searching his face.

"Um. Fine?" Leo said. He wasn't sure what she wanted to hear, or what she was really asking. "I mean…he rescued me. He's been taking care of me. He…seems nice?"

Nice. Ha. How about: devastatingly attractive, in a monosyllabic, mysterious mountain man sort of way. Leo hoped he wasn't blushing, or that if he was, Dr Ogilvy would take it for a minor fever.

Watching Kirk walk into his bedroom had been a real shock.

Leo must have been out of his head with pain, to think of him as some kind of hairy monster. Though Kirk did have a wild mane of dark curls; now that he was clean-shaven, the contrast between the strong, spare line of his jaw and the riot of curly hair was even more striking. Leo was longing to untie it again, to sink his hands into it.

Dr Ogilvy stroked her chin. "I think you should stay here for the time being."

Oh, Leo mouthed soundlessly. He hadn't really considered his immediate future yet.

He'd been too busy thinking about his leg, about how easily he could have died out there in the wilds. What a miracle it was to have survived this: to have been found, in all that lonely wilderness, by the one man who could free him from that horrible trap.

"If you prefer, I could get you transport to the nearest hospital," Dr Ogilvy said, looking at him sharply. "But I know they're short of beds, and what you really need is a couple days' rest while your leg heals up. Stay in bed today, and tomorrow you might get up for some hours if you feel better. Mind you, that's only if you can manage to avoid putting too much weight on your leg or jarring it. You can practice that here at the cabin, all you need is some crutches. And, between you and me—" she leaned over and said in Leo's ear, "Kirk could use the company. I worry about that boy. He's alone too much."

Leo stifled a laugh.

"Ma'am," he said, lowering his voice, "That *boy* is a six-foot behemoth with legs like trees and a chin you could use for a chisel."

"Really? I hadn't noticed." Dr Ogilvy's eyes

twinkled. "He wasn't that big when I delivered him. Good thing, too."

Leo laughed, then groaned as his stomach muscles protested.

"Good," Dr Ogilvy said, eyeing him. "Laughter is good, even if it hurts. I'm sure you'll feel better tomorrow. But you take care of yourself, boy, and if you run into trouble, call me."

After that, Leo couldn't protest against her calling him *boy*. Not if she did it to Kirk, too.

He spent most of that day waking and sleeping, dreaming odd feverish dreams that he couldn't recall when he woke up. If Kirk was nearby, he didn't show himself, to Leo's badly hidden disappointment.

By evening, he was feeling a little more like himself. His leg still ached fiercely, and the rest of his body felt sore and stiff, but his head was getting clearer. And he felt hungry, for the first time since he'd woken up in these unfamiliar surroundings.

His stomach rumbled, and he wondered if he could get out of bed, see if this place had a kitchen. He still had a lot of supplies in his backpack; it would be a nice way to pay Kirk back, at least a little, if he could cook for him.

When he tried to swing his leg out of bed, it gave such an agonizing twinge that he cried out, though he hastily tried to muffle it.

"Okay, bad idea," he told himself. "No cooking for *you*."

Then the bedroom door opened and Kirk walked in, carrying a tray with two dark blue bowls on it.

"Doc says you should stay in bed," Kirk told him, in that deep, slightly hoarse voice that was so disturbingly attractive.

"Yeah," Leo said, chagrined. He tucked his aching leg back under the blankets. "She's not wrong."

He looked up at Kirk. "She said I should stay here and heal up for a couple days. Is that okay—I mean, do you want me to stay? I could call the hospital-"

Leo cringed as soon as the words left his mouth. Good god, he sounded like a needy teenager.

Kirk put the tray down on the bedside table.

"It's fine," he said curtly, then gestured to the

tray. "Got you something to eat."

Leo shook his head, a little frustrated. "No, seriously, tell me. I don't want to be a burden, and I don't even know—am I taking up your bed?"

Kirk's dark eyebrows rose just a fraction. "No. This is the guest room."

Leo slumped back against the pillows. "Oh. Good." He felt obscurely disappointed.

Then he looked at the bowls. Something dark and ruddy that looked like a vegetable soup, and something dark and murky that he couldn't make out at all.

"Thanks for the food, um. What is it?"

Kirk was very hard to read, but now his strong jaw seemed to tense a little. "Left one's beet soup, the other's venison stew."

Leo stared at the two bowls, nonplussed. Soup for the invalid, huh?

"Okay. Sounds good." *Better if I could bake some corn bread to go with it…no, let's not think about that right now.*

Then he realized what he was missing, and

smiled up at Kirk. "Can I have a spoon?"

Kirk looked completely surprised for just a second, and it was wonderful. His dark eyes opened wider, and his mouth lost a little of its tension. He looked much more open and friendly, and Leo almost mourned when the look faded and his expression closed down again.

"Sorry," Kirk said, gruffly. "Not used to visitors."

As his host left the room, Leo bit back various smart-ass remarks along the lines of *Really? I never would have guessed, you seem so sociable.*

Quite apart from the fact that he owed Kirk his life, it wasn't fair to judge him so harshly. Kirk clearly was sociable enough to let Leo stay in his house. Cabin. Whatever.

And Leo...Leo *really* wanted to be sociable in return. As much as Kirk would let him. Which probably didn't extend to letting Leo kiss him.

But as Leo began to spoon venison stew into his mouth, he imagined it anyway.

Kirk was going crazy. That wasn't an exaggeration, that was pure brutal fact.

There was a delicious-smelling, gorgeous young man in his territory, all *over* his territory, asking him questions and opening kitchen drawers and generally making a nuisance of himself, when he wasn't tripping over his own crutches.

It was disturbing. It was exasperating. It was *noisy*.

What Kirk was used to was silence. The wind in the trees, bird calls, maybe a plane overhead once in a while.

Silence wherever he turned, silence from morning to night. Nothing to mark the passing of time except his own heartbeat and the wheeling of the sun.

Now, the cabin felt suddenly alive.

Kirk's wolf blood itched in his veins, making him acutely aware of everything Leo's presence was doing to him.

Leo's scent was everywhere, enticing him, drawing him in until he had to clench his hands into fists to keep from sniffing the back of the young man's neck. *Don't even think about licking it.*

And there was the simple awareness of his existence—the warm, alive sensation of another human being, so close to him, occupying the same space. The sound of his breathing, his heartbeat. The way he hummed under his breath every now and then, so softly that it would be barely audible to normal ears.

"Hey, where do you keep the—oh never mind, found it," Leo said cheerfully behind him.

Kirk kept staring out the window so he wouldn't find himself staring at Leo, instead. Or worse still, putting his hands on him.

It was a beautiful fall day, with a bright morning sun painting the birch leaves bright gold. There would be rain from the east later, though; he could smell it, the moisture hanging heavy on the wind.

Behind him, Leo stood by the old pot-bellied stove. He was making breakfast.

Kirk had no idea what he was cooking. It smelled interesting, but he couldn't identify the scent at all; if anything, it reminded him of cookies, which didn't seem possible.

To Kirk, breakfast meant a bowl of cereal and milk, or if he was coming up on the change, maybe some dried meat and a bowl of water. It didn't involve pans or spices or wooden spoons.

"Nearly done," Leo said behind him.

There was a clatter that Kirk recognized instinctively: Leo had dropped one of his crutches.

Faster than thought, Kirk spun around and grabbed the thing as it fell, then lodged it back under Leo's arm.

Leo was giving him that wide-eyed look again. It wasn't the look Kirk was familiar with from others, the *you are a freak* look. This was a look of wonder, and he didn't know how to deal with it.

"Nice reflexes," Leo said.

Kirk grunted, feeling awkward. He couldn't be

proud of anything that belonged to the wolf. And by now, he wasn't even sure how much of him was left that *didn't* belong to the wolf.

"Not really a morning person, are you?" Leo said. He seemed to take it in stride that Kirk didn't answer him half the time; apparently he just liked to make conversation, even if he was the only one contributing.

It was true that mornings could be a trial. Now that winter was coming, the wolf in him was awake during the day as well as the night. It meant snatching a couple hours' sleep here and there, before the restless urges of the wolf jerked him awake again.

Kirk eyed what Leo was doing by the stove, curiosity overcoming his need to keep himself away.

Leo was using one of Kirk's old cast-iron pans, and he was frying…oats? In butter?

It smelled amazing, warm and hearty, and the scent really did remind him of cookies. Oatmeal cookies.

Kirk hadn't eaten those in a long time.

The oats were turning brown, and Leo stirred them vigorously with his wooden spoon.

"Fried oats?" Kirk asked at last, trying not to sound too doubtful. He didn't see how that could possibly be edible, no matter how good it smelled.

Leo smiled at him over his shoulder, still stirring busily. His smiles came so easily, so freely.

"Old recipe," he said. "Don't worry, I'm not done yet."

The butter was slowly vanishing, absorbing into the oats. The smell grew richer.

"Hand me that jug, will you?" Leo said.

Bemused, Kirk handed him the earthenware jug and watched as Leo poured water into the pan, the first drops fizzing and sputtering on the hot surface.

It looked like oatmeal soup now. No—oatmeal porridge, Kirk realized. The real thing, not the instant version.

"Now I just need to bring it up to a boil and keep stirring for some time," Leo told him. "This is kind of the boring part."

Out of nowhere came the thought, *I could make it entertaining for you.*

Kirk could sink to his knees right in front of

Leo, peel off the faded sweatpants that barely clung to his hips, suck him down fast and hard until he began to moan...

Kirk breathed in harshly, suppressing the fantasy. *You're his host, and even if you're a monster, he doesn't have to know it,* he told himself. *Control yourself.*

"Do you have any cream?" Leo asked him.

For a moment, Kirk couldn't find enough breath to reply. Then he realized what Leo was asking him. *Goddamn it, get your mind out of the gutter!*

He shook his head. He didn't stock much more than the basics.

"Oh well, it's not necessary. Tasty, though," Leo said. He licked his lips unconsciously, as if remembering the taste of that cream.

Kirk looked away hastily, though he couldn't make himself move entirely out of Leo's way. He kept standing near the stove, his heartbeat loud and fast in his own ears, and tried to ignore the heavy press of his cock against the inner seam of his jeans.

Leo hummed again under his breath as he stirred the porridge vigorously.

"My grandmother has a special wooden spoon she uses just for this," he said. He wasn't speaking to Kirk directly, or at least not looking at him directly. Giving him space. "She calls it a spirtle. I've never heard anyone use that word except her. She may have made it up."

"I've heard it," Kirk said, surprising himself.

Leo looked up, his blue eyes bright in the slanting morning sunshine. "Yeah?"

"It's Scottish," Kirk said. He felt the space between them yawning like a crevasse, ready to be filled with words. Or touches. Or—no.

Words weren't easy, but they were safe. Safer.

"My mother was a Scotswoman," Kirk said reluctantly. "A MacDougall."

"MacDougall," Leo repeated, slowly, as if tasting the word for flavor. "That's lovely."

Leo's eyes brightened with what Kirk was beginning to recognize as mischief. "So do you have a kilt?"

Kirk shook his head. His mother's parents had emigrated to the New World trying to leave the Old

World behind them, not recreate it, and they had cut as many ties as they could, including their ties to the clan. Kirk wondered, sometimes, about the family they had left behind.

"Pity," Leo said, with a small sigh. Then he looked away, a flush rising on his cheekbones, and began to stir so vigorously that the porridge nearly slopped out of the pan.

Kirk watched him, all his senses alert. The scent that was all Leo mingled with the rich warm scent of the oatmeal, and he knew his mouth was watering.

"There's a clan tartan, though," he said grudgingly, trying to distract himself. Or distract Leo, he wasn't sure. "A clan motto, castles, all that. My mother told me."

Leo blew out a long breath. "Castles, huh." His eyes lit up. "So what's the motto?"

Kirk scratched the emerging bristles on his chin, while he tried to remember how to pronounce the words.

"*Buaidh no bàs,*" he said at last.

Leo nearly dropped his spoon. "Wow. That

sounds…I don't know…epic. Like a battle cry."

Kirk nodded. "It is. *Conquer or Die.*"

"Wow," Leo said again, but it didn't sound like he was mocking Kirk.

He stirred counterclockwise, poking at lumps of oats with his spoon until they fell apart. "This should be nearly done. Do we have any honey?"

Kirk tried not to notice the 'we'. *It's just a manner of speech; no need to feel so pleased,* he told himself.

"Think so," he said, and began to rummage through the storage bins. At least honey didn't go off; if he had any, it was probably very old, but it should be okay.

"Some people eat porridge with just salt," Leo said. "Personally, I believe in honey and as much cream as the bowl will hold."

"Could be your motto," Kirk said, coming up with a jar of dark honey from the very bottom of the bin.

Leo blinked at him, his eyes bright with mischief. "Was that a joke? Whoa, hold the phone, first you said more than three words this morning and now you're making jokes?"

Kirk scowled at him, but Leo wasn't daunted at all. He just smiled, a smile of such incandescent sweetness that Kirk found himself blinking as if he'd been hit on the head.

"You're right, that could totally be my motto," Leo said, still smiling. "Get myself a crest with a bowl of creamy oatmeal, crossed by a wooden spoon, surmounted by a crown of stars."

"Stars," Kirk said, not quite a question.

This was possibly the silliest conversation he'd ever had, so why was he enjoying it so much? He hated small talk, always had. Not least because small talk meant nosy, impertinent questions, questions he couldn't begin to answer. But Leo's questions weren't quite like that.

Leo nodded and intoned, "Stars of deliciousness." He held the wooden spoon aloft dramatically. "This oatmeal is done."

Kirk set the table with blue earthenware bowls and metal spoons, plus the jar of honey.

Leo spooned the oatmeal into the bowls, then

added honey. It had crystallized into great sugary lumps, but it melted quickly enough into the hot porridge.

They ate, and Kirk tried not to watch Leo licking his spoon with long swipes of his pink tongue.

The oatmeal was good. *Better* than good.

Kirk was quietly amazed: how could something so simple, with so few ingredients, taste so good? He'd always thought that real cooking involved a lot of hard-to-find ingredients and complicated techniques with French names.

"Nice to cook on a proper stove again," Leo said in between spoonfuls. "I hate my camping stove. I thought it was a good idea to pick the smallest lightweight option, but it's so flimsy it keeps falling over."

Not an experienced hiker, then. That wasn't a surprise; Leo's backpack looked fairly new, too.

Kirk scraped the last spoonfuls out of the bowl, then settled back in his chair with a sigh. The old wooden chair creaked with his weight.

"That was very good, Leo," said Leo, with ironic emphasis. "Where did you learn to cook like that, Leo? Would you like to do it some more, because all I can do is open cans, and besides, you owe me."

Kirk stared at his guest. "You don't owe me," he said firmly.

Strangely, Leo frowned at this, his shoulders slumping just a fraction. "Well. I think I do owe you. Call me crazy, but I like being alive."

"You were lucky," Kirk said. He didn't know how else to say it, how to explain it, but he didn't want Leo to feel indebted to him. He didn't want Leo doing him *favors*. And as for saving his life…how could he have done anything else? *I've hurt enough people.*

"You said that before," Leo said, still frowning. "So okay, I was lucky. But you're still the one who saved me, and I'm not going to forget it."

Kirk didn't know what to say to that, either, so he fell back on his old standby: silence.

Leo licked the last bit of honey from his spoon. "I notice you're not denying my assessment of your cooking skills, though."

Kirk snorted. "Nothing wrong with canned soup."

Opening cans for dinner was a perfectly acceptable way to live, as far as he was concerned. They sold those cans in the millions, didn't they? Someone had to buy them. And they tasted okay. Not jaw-droppingly amazing, no, but okay. Better than MREs, for one thing.

Of course, the wolf didn't open cans. The wolf ate raw meat, or smoked, or dried. But the wolf didn't rule him to that extent, not yet. He would cling to his humanity while he could.

"I hate to challenge your convictions," Leo said airily. "But if you're willing to do the shopping, I will make borscht for dinner, and it's going to rock your world, my friend."

My friend. Kirk swallowed.

For a moment, it felt like a door was opening.

A door into a world where he was just a lonely man living in the woods, who had gained a new friend. Someone he could talk to. Someone he could, perhaps, even love.

But the wolf didn't care about love. The wolf only cared about three things: eating, fighting, and fucking.

Kirk could not let Leo encounter the wolf. And yet he couldn't bring himself to ask Leo to leave.

There was only one other solution he was willing to entertain.

Leo let the spoon drop back in the bowl with a satisfied sigh of his own. "Even without cream, that was awesome."

He stretched, his t-shirt riding up a little to expose the soft skin of his belly, and Kirk tried very hard not to stare.

"I have to admit, I don't really mind that my hiking trip wasn't a big success," Leo said.

He pushed the spoon around in the bowl, staring at it with unfocused eyes. "I thought hiking would be a fun adventure, that it would help me get my thoughts back on track. But it was more like a very stressful...I don't know, business trip."

Kirk blinked. "Business trip?" he repeated.

"Yeah," Leo said. "Having to stay in focus all the time, no time to relax. Check the map, check the weather, make sure your gear stays dry, don't get too cold, don't get too hot, hide your food from bears, check the map again..." He shook his head ruefully.

"And then I still got in trouble."

Kirk chuckled at the comically mournful expression on Leo's face. "I see."

Leo was shoving his chair back, maneuvering with his crutches to help him stand up. It was an awkward business, but Kirk let him deal with the crutches on his own. He wouldn't insult Leo by trying to help unless it was clearly necessary.

"Wow, I reek," Leo said, almost to himself. He sniffed his armpit demonstratively, then lifted his gaze to meet Kirk's, a humorous plea in his eyes.

Kirk couldn't look away. God, what was Leo doing to him? Did he even know he was doing it? Did he have any idea that by lifting his arm like that, he was wafting his maddeningly alluring scent in Kirk's direction, as bold and brazen as a woman arching her back to display her cleavage?

No, of course he didn't know. Kirk had to keep reminding himself of that. Leo *couldn't* know what he was doing to Kirk. And that was just as it should be.

"I'll run you a bath," Kirk said reluctantly.

God help me.

Leo shuffled slowly into the bathroom, careful not to let the crutches slip on the smooth tile.

The bathroom was larger than he had expected. It was old, like the rest of the cabin, and the claw-footed tub must have been an antique even when it was first installed. There was a toilet with a wooden seat, but no shower.

If he wanted to get clean, it was the bath or nothing.

Leo eyed the steaming water with some trepidation. He longed for a bath, but how was he ever going to get in there without jarring his leg, or getting the bandages wet?

On the wall to his left hung a metal towel rail, but it was too far from the bath. And if he put any weight on it, he'd probably rip the thing off the wall.

"You can prop up your foot here," Kirk said behind him. "Keep it out of the water."

Leo jumped, nearly dropping his crutches. He couldn't help being startled. For such a big man, Kirk was very light on his feet.

"Here, where?" he asked, trying to recover his cool.

Kirk moved past him and pointed out a wooden rack that lay across the foot of the bath. It was the kind of thing you could put your drink on, or some soap and a brush, or maybe a book, so you could reach it while you were lying in the water.

For a moment, Leo was distracted by a mental image of Kirk lying in the bath: gloriously naked, his hair streaming wetly over his shoulders, soap bubbles sliding down his muscular chest...

He shook himself. *Don't start to fantasize about the man while he's trying to help you, for god's sake.*

Keeping his eyes on the wooden rack, he tried to imagine how this idea of Kirk's was going to work, and shook his head dubiously. "Prop my leg up," he said. "Right. That still doesn't solve the problem of actually getting into the bath in the first place."

Then he looked up at Kirk, suddenly flushing with embarrassment. "Sorry," he said quickly. "I shoot my mouth off a lot, and I don't mean to. You've been so good to me—"

"Easy," Kirk said in his deep, rough voice. He paused, looking down at Leo, and Leo thought he could see a faint hint of a flush along his cheekbones.

"I can help," Kirk said. "Or I can ask Dr Ogilvy to send up a nurse."

Leo shook his head violently. "No nurse."

There was no room for a nurse in the cabin; he was overcrowding Kirk as it was. Also, he didn't want a stranger stepping in between them, a stranger who would almost certainly drive Kirk back into his monosyllabic shell.

And since Kirk was offering to help him get into the bath—well. Leo wasn't going to look a gift horse in the mouth.

Awkwardly, Leo sat down on the closed seat of the toilet, dropping his crutches onto the floor.

Taking his shirt off was easy; taking his sweatpants off, not so much, even though he'd dug them from his backpack because of their relaxed fit. When he bent down to get the pants over his injured leg, his muscles protested so much that he had to stop and sit up again, his head spinning.

"Let me," Kirk said, and as if it was nothing out of the ordinary, he knelt down in front of Leo and put his big, warm hands on Leo's leg.

Leo bit his lip.

It would not *be a good idea to get a hard-on right now*, he told himself. *Absolutely* not. *Don't even think about it. Don't think about what he's doing. Don't even look at him.*

But he *had* to look. He had to watch as Kirk's hands lifted his aching leg, drawing the sweatpants down his calf until his leg was free.

Kirk's hands were so warm, and his touch was surprisingly gentle. His head was bent, and his dark hair spilled wildly down his shoulders, barely constrained by a leather tie in the middle.

Now Kirk's hands were gripping the hem of his boxer shorts, drawing them down.

Leo forgot to breathe.

He knew he was half-hard without looking; he could feel the heat in his lower body, the tingling pleasure of Kirk's touch only increasing his agitation.

But Kirk didn't say anything. He just sniffed

audibly, and dropped Leo's boxers on the floor.

Oh man, did he smell that bad?

"Sorry," Leo said hurriedly. "I really do need a bath, don't I."

"No need to apologize," Kirk told him. He got up from his kneeling position in one flowing, supple move that Leo tried very hard not to admire.

"Stand up on your good leg," Kirk said, and Leo hurried to obey, teetering on one leg until Kirk steadied him.

"I'm going to lift you into the bath," Kirk told him. "Just relax."

Leo tried to relax, he really did, and it worked much better than he would have thought.

Mostly, it went so well because of Kirk. Leo felt like an awkward weight, with limbs sticking out in all directions, but Kirk didn't even seem to be breathing hard. The size of his biceps wasn't just for show; it felt as though he could have lifted Leo in one hand. But both his hands were clamped under Leo's arms as he maneoeuvred him toward the bath.

"Lift your left leg up, put it on the rack," Kirk

said.

Leo nearly kicked the rack to the floor on his first try, but the second time he managed to wedge his wounded leg on top. His stomach muscles complained, but he held the position as Kirk slowly lowered him into the water.

"Hot, hot, hot," Leo chanted as the water closed over his right leg. "Tsss, hot, I'm going to be boiled like a lobster but at least I'll be a clean lobster—"

Kirk paused, holding him steady half out of the water, his eyebrows rising just a fraction.

Leo laughed. "Sorry, no, keep going, it's not too hot, just—hsss—needs getting used to. Oh god, that feels amazing." He knew he was babbling, but he had to cover for himself, for the tell-tale flush on his cheeks, his twitching cock. It wasn't the hot water that was doing that to him, but his awareness of Kirk's strong hands holding him up.

Deeper and deeper he went, until his behind hit the porcelain bottom of the tub. Then Kirk let go, and if Leo sighed a little, he hoped it went unheard.

Oh, but the hot water was such a good idea. Leo leaned back into the glorious steamy water, feeling his skin tingle and flush.

"So good," he chanted, half to himself.

There was a sliver of soap on the wooden rack, and if he leaned forward he could just reach it. He stretched and managed to grab it on the first try. The soap smelled like lavender, and he hummed under his breath as he began to work up a lather.

Then, from the corner of his eye, he saw Kirk turning away, clearly preparing to leave him alone in his sudsy bliss.

"Won't you stay?" Leo said. "You should probably make sure I don't drown in the bath. Terrible thing to happen." He let his voice drop into a nasal announcer's drawl. "Stranger found drowned in bath; local resident Kirk Anderson accused of negligence. Asked for details, Mr Anderson shrugged. "*It happens,*" he said."

Kirk shook his head, but Leo was watching carefully, and he saw a corner of Kirk's mouth curl up, just for a second.

Yes! Made you smile. Next thing you know I'll make you laugh so hard you get a bellyache, he promised himself. Hey, it was good to have ambitions. Even impossible ones.

Kirk sat down on the closed wooden toilet seat,

settled his broad shoulders against the tiled wall, and closed his eyes. It was hard to tell if he was protecting Leo's modesty or just taking a nap.

Leo sang softly to himself as he soaped up his arms, then dunked them into the water. "*Au claire de la lune, mon ami Pierrot...*" It was an old song from his childhood, and he had no idea why it had popped up into his head just now.

Maybe it was something to do with feeling warm, safe, and protected.

He sank back into the warm water, the old song unspooling in his head until he reached: "*Ouvre-moi ta porte, pour l'amour de Dieu.*"

This he sang very softly, and if he looked at Kirk while he sang it, there was no one to see him do it.

Kirk drove down the long winding dirt road that led to the main road to Sevenacres, feeling strange and unsettled. He never came to town this close to the change.

Just take precautions, he told himself. *Move slow. Don't growl at people.*

Strangely enough, he hadn't wanted to growl at Leo so far. But then, Leo...Leo was special.

Every instinct Kirk possessed said that Leo wasn't an intruder upon his territory; Leo was welcome. Leo should be protected, kept safe.

He knew what it meant.

He had known before he lifted a naked, warm, willing Leo into his arms. That was only the last drop in a bucket full of impossible desires.

He wanted to take Leo as his mate.

Was it just the wolf, reacting to that alluring scent, that lithe young body? Or was it more than that?

He shook his head, dark curls flying around his ears. He couldn't think about that, not now. The only thing he was sure of was that Leo did need to be protected.

Because the change was coming, and the wolf didn't care about human scruples.

If the wolf wanted a mate, he took one.

Kirk parked the truck across from the Corner Store.

It wasn't the main grocery store in Sevenacres anymore, now that a huge supermarket had opened just out of town, but Kirk preferred to shop locally. On days like this, he couldn't deal with the cacophony of sights, sounds, and smells in the big supermarket anyway.

The bell over the door jangled as Kirk walked in, and he was careful to shut the door quietly behind him.

"Good morning, Mr Anderson," Joan Grayson said, smiling warmly at him from behind the counter. Her hands were busy in a complicated motion, almost too fast to see, as she crocheted yet another scarf in bright colors to add to the collection in the window. The scarves sold like hotcakes to tourists in the leaf season, and clearly she was trying to get as much stock ready as she could.

"Morning," he said. He grabbed a basket and began to assemble the ingredients for borscht, glancing down now and again at the list Leo had given him.

It felt almost absurdly domestic. He was shopping with a list, given to him by—*no. Leo is not your boyfriend. Don't go down that path. Don't fool yourself. Leo is just a houseguest, a stranger who's staying with you until his leg heals up.*

It was strangely difficult to remember that.

Beets, cabbage, onion, garlic, sour cream...beef. Apparently Leo needed raw beef for this soup. That would be a challenge.

Kirk walked over to the meat section, the basket dangling from one hand. At least the meat was pre-packaged, and he didn't have to stand there and watch a butcher dismantle a whole carcass, while trying to restrain himself from leaping the counter and ripping fresh steaks from the animal's flank with his teeth.

When he lifted the package of beef from the cooler, it didn't smell as good as freshly killed prey; the meat was dead, and the blood-scent was metallic and old. Still, the water ran into his mouth. He wanted to chew open the package.

Hurriedly, he dropped the meat into the basket and walked on.

He had all the ingredients Leo had asked for, now he was just adding extras: apples, some oranges, other things he thought Leo might like, as well as a generous supply of staples.

Leo would have to fend for himself for a few days. He must not run out of food.

Kirk turned on his heel and walked back to the dairy section to look for a carton of fresh cream. *As much cream as the bowl will hold*, Leo's cheerful tenor said in his mind.

That would never be Kirk's motto, even if it didn't put filthy thoughts into his head.

As far as Kirk's life was concerned, his bowl was empty. And if he thought he could fill it up, he was just fooling himself.

When he completed his circuit of the Corner

Store, the basket was full to overflowing. He should probably have grabbed a cart, instead, but he hated walking behind those; their wheels squeaked so loudly, and they moved so clumsily and slowly, like geese.

Another image that belonged to the wolf, that Kirk would just as soon forget: feathers and blood, soaking into the snow.

"My, do you have plans?" Joan said brightly as she rang up his groceries. "Are you making something special for your houseguest?"

Kirk looked up, surprised.

She laughed when she saw his expression. "Oh come now, you know Dr Ogilvy wouldn't keep a juicy bit of news like that to herself. She said you saved his life, is that true?"

Judiciously, Kirk nodded.

Joan's smile grew wider. "What a good thing you found him," she said, merrily juggling packages of oats and dried fruit as she bagged them one by one. "Imagine getting caught in one of those horrible old bear traps. Those things are a menace, I've always said so."

Her voice ran on, musical as a mountain

stream, but it was soon drowned out by a huge roaring noise from outside the store.

Kirk whipped around, staring. He could feel his lips drawing back in a snarl.

The noise only grew louder, and now a horrible smell reached his nostrils. Gasoline, exhaust fumes, leather, sweat...and something else.

Something that made the short hairs at the back of his neck stand up.

"Oh, drat those motorcycles," Joan was saying. "Such a lovely day today, why can't they take a walk instead, or rent a bicycle next door?"

More motorcycles roared past the store, at least twenty of them, their riders clad in black leather and wearing mirrored helmets.

Tourists, of course, Kirk told himself, trying to breathe slowly, trying to get his heartbeat back to normal.

It wasn't as though he'd never seen tourists on motorcycles before. Most of them were dentists or accountants or something else boring and respectable; men who loved to put on leather in the weekends, lower their voices, call each other by silly macho names, and pretend they were in a gang.

But it didn't feel the same. The roar of the motorcycles faded away into the distance, but Kirk could still taste the scent of them in the air. It tasted like danger. Like challenge.

This is why it's a bad idea to go into town this close to full moon, he thought grimly. It felt as though the wolf was snarling inside him, trying to get out. He couldn't trust his own reactions anymore.

"I can see you don't like them either," Joan said, while she wrapped up the last of his groceries. "Horrible noise, isn't it?"

Kirk nodded, drawing himself up in a tight, straight line. It was an effort to compose himself; he kept wanting to drop his jaw and bare his teeth.

Hurriedly, he paid and left, but as soon as the door of the Corner Store closed behind him, the scent of the motorcyclists hit him again, stronger now that he was out in the open.

It was incredibly difficult to ignore, but he managed it, carrying the sacks of groceries to his truck. *Act like a normal person doing the shopping*, he told himself firmly. *Not like someone with claws itching behind his fingernails.*

Kirk dropped the last sack into the back of the truck and turned on his heel.

He had one last purchase to make.

There was no one in the hardware store except Mr Quint, the owner. He was a small, wizened man who always had a cigarette dangling from the corner of his mouth, though he didn't light it inside the store.

Kirk walked straight to the spools of chain. They hung in rows, neatly sorted by thickness and strength. He unspooled a length, tugging at it to test it. If it broke, of course, he'd have to reimburse Mr Quint; he felt the man's sharp eyes on his back, watching him.

"You worried about security, now?" Mr Quint asked him casually. "Didn't think your cabin even had a lock."

"It doesn't," Kirk answered shortly. "This is for my boat."

"Ah, your boat," Mr Quint said, and nothing more.

Kirk tried to ignore those sharp eyes measuring him. Mr Quint knew as well as he did that Kirk's fishing boat was nothing to write home about—it was old, it needed a good coat of fresh paint, and it lay docked at the old rowhouse by Windmere lake, where nobody had disturbed it for months. It wasn't the kind of property anyone was likely to steal.

Kirk gave the chain another surreptitious tug. It had to be strong enough to hold the wolf. He didn't think it would.

He unwound another length of chain from a spool on the bottom shelf. An industrial chain. The links were thick and heavy in his hands.

"Titanium reinforced, that one is," Mr Quint told him, ostentatiously sweeping some barely visible wood shavings into a corner of the store. "Guaranteed for life not to rust or break."

"I'll take it," Kirk said.

He lifted a snap lock, heavy and solid, like the chain. "This guaranteed too?"

"Sure," Mr Quint said. "Though not against hacksaws or anything. Just rust."

Kirk nodded.

It wasn't perfect, but there was no perfect security that would hold a werewolf. Nothing he'd ever found, anyway.

There was one item he already owned, that he had bought in another town where nobody knew him: a dog collar. Made from thick, heavy bridle leather, it was a collar that would hold even a dangerous, aggressive dog. Or a wolf.

He paid for the lock and chain and left the store, still feeling Mr Quint's eyes pricking into his back.

Leo was starting to feel chilly, but he wouldn't leave his seat on the porch to find warmer clothing.

The view was too glorious.

The sun was setting, slipping slowly down into a bed of clouds, and the sky shaded from orange to a purple so vivid it could have been a crayon color.

If I painted this, it would look cheap, Leo thought. He could just see it: the sun setting over the pines in a riot of oil paint color, like an oversaturated photograph or a cheap souvenir postcard. *Why does it never look cheap when nature does it?*

He hadn't found an answer to that yet when he heard the muted sound of Kirk's truck, slowly chugging up the long, steep drive to the cabin. The truck sounded bad-tempered, like an old and ornery dog.

Of course Kirk would have a truck like that, Leo thought, trying to repress an absurdly fond smile. It was probably ancient and only held together by endless repairs.

It seemed to be Kirk's natural role to fix things. Or people.

The truck coughed up the driveway and stopped.

Leo suddenly felt a little strange, sitting here on the porch with his crutches leaning against the porch railing. Like he was waiting for Kirk to come home. *Hi, honey, how was your day?*

Well, he *was* waiting, he acknowledged to himself. Watching the sunset was just a bonus. But it felt...presumptuous?

As if asking him to help you in and out of the bath wasn't presumptuous, a sharp, unpleasant voice grumbled in his head.

Kirk jumped out of the truck, landing so smoothly that his long legs hit the ground without an audible thud.

That was another thing about Kirk that Leo found fascinating: despite his size, he could move so quietly, like a big cat.

With a nod to Leo, Kirk began to unload sacks of groceries from the truck. His flannel shirtsleeves were rolled up to the elbow, and Leo watched the play of muscle in his forearms until he realized that he was staring.

Now Leo really felt presumptuous, sitting here like a lord of the manor while Kirk did all the work.

He reached tentatively for his crutches—

"Stay there," Kirk said.

It sounded so gruff, but when Kirk's dark eyes met his, it wasn't anger Leo saw there, but warmth.

The power of that look was so strong it felt physical, like an electric shock. For a moment, Leo stopped breathing.

He fell back into the wooden chair, trying to restrain his heart from hammering its way out of his chest.

Holy crap.

It was as though he'd been walking around deaf and blind all this time, and suddenly a thunderclap had opened his eyes and cleared his vision.

While Leo slumped back into the chair, Kirk strode into the cabin, two bags in each arm, and the screen door swung shut behind him.

Leo stared blindly at the sunset.

I'm in love with him.

It was more than just physical attraction, as he'd thought at first.

It explained everything: why Leo wanted so much to get to know Kirk better, find out everything there was to know about him. Why he wanted to cook for Kirk—sure, Leo loved cooking, it was one of his favorite activities, but mostly he wanted Kirk to appreciate his cooking. He wanted Kirk to smile at him, even if it was only one corner of his mouth turning up a fraction.

Then reality came crashing back in on him.

You're in love with a loner who lives in a remote cabin and barely speaks two words to you in an hour, that same acerbic, deeply unsentimental voice told him. *And if you tell him you're gay, he'll probably kick your ass down the mountain. Get real.*

Leo didn't like this voice much, but it lived in his head anyway. It might be his conscience, though truth be told, it sounded more like his dad.

Leo's dad Theodore was a sharp-tongued, sharp-faced man who was very good at his job—he was a research chemist for a major cosmetics company— and deeply unappreciative of his son's choices in life. Their last conversation before Leo left on his hiking trip was still etched upon his mind.

"Painting, hah! Cooking, hah! Art student, hah! What you need, my boy, is a steady job and a sensible woman to take care of you. And don't give me that crap about how you're *gay* now. I remember how you used to go steady with that Evelyn. You were head over heels in love."

"Dad. I was *seven*."

"So you had more sense at seven than you do now. This is a surprise?"

"Dad..." Leo sighed.

He knew it was hopeless, but he still wanted his dad to understand.

Two years of chemistry at college had been enough to convince Leo that he would never follow in his dad's footsteps. He wanted to be an artist. Not the kind of artist who played around, like some of the trust fund kids he'd met since he'd switched to art school. No, he wanted to be the kind of artist who *worked* at it, who made money at it and didn't have to hang on his parent for support.

And most of all, he wanted his dad to acknowledge that he was gay.

He'd been trying to talk to his dad about all of this for three years now. It wasn't going so well.

Theodore shook his head sharply. "So this year you're gay, next year you'll be straight again, the year after you'll probably come and tell me you're a lesbian. Whatever. I don't care and I don't want to hear about it until you've sorted out your life."

"I'm not going to get married, Dad," Leo said, trying to keep his voice calm and level. "At least...not to a woman. If that's part of what 'sorting out my life' means to you, it's never going to happen."

Theodore waved a dismissive hand. "Yeah, yeah, so you say now. Just you wait until you find the right woman. I never knew what I wanted either, until I found your mother."

That was too much, and Leo felt his own temper rising abruptly, like a kettle coming to a boil. "Dad! I know what I want, okay? You're the one who can't accept that."

"Is that so?" Theodore asked, suddenly thrusting his nose forward. He was so tense he was almost quivering, like a hunting dog coming upon a scent. "You know what you want, do you? Well. Tell me, then. I wait to be enlightened."

The sarcasm was so heavy it practically melted the varnish off the table, and Leo could feel himself flushing. He cursed his fair skin and his father's uncanny ability to get a rise out of him.

"I don't want a safe, steady job," Leo told him, trying hard to keep his voice level. "I don't want to work at the same lab for forty years until they retire me. I want to paint, and I want to make a living as a painter. If I can't do that, I'll work as a cook and paint on the side." He took a deep breath. "And I want a boyfriend who loves me as much as I love him. Someone I can build a life with. But I haven't found him yet. Do you want to hear about it when I do?"

For a moment, this silenced even Theodore.

They stared at each other, Theodore's gray eyes meeting Leo's blue ones.

"Goddamn it," Theodore said then, surprising Leo. His dad didn't swear often. "You're just like your mother, even now. After all I did to install some sense into you."

Leo smiled, though it didn't come easy. "I take that as a compliment."

"You would," his dad said sourly. "Well, go and stick your head into a pot of paint then, if you have to. But don't come crying to me when you run out of money and your so-called friends break your heart and wreck your car, okay?"

"Okay," Leo said slowly. *Break your heart and wreck your car.* Yeah, that summed up his dad's priorities all right.

He'd kept his word. His reserves hadn't quite run out yet—it was hard to spend a lot of money while hiking, and most of his hiking gear was borrowed— but he was definitely getting there. He had sold a few paintings, but mostly to friends, and there was a limit to that market.

Maybe he could find a job at a restaurant in the town below. It was a small town, from what he could see from above, but they must have tourists, so presumably they had restaurants.

And then when his shift was over, he could bike up to the cabin, have a late supper with Kirk...

Stop dreaming, that same voice told him sharply. *Kirk doesn't want you to stay. He's just being polite, but really he's waiting until he can kick you out and go back to being a mountain hermit again.*

Leo shook his head.

That look in Kirk's eyes...he hadn't imagined that.

There was something growing between them, and if it was only the tentative beginnings of friendship and not love, then he would still take it.

He'd take anything Kirk wanted to give him.

Kirk sat at the old kitchen table, chopping onions.

It wasn't the easiest task in the world for a man who was holding onto his humanity by his fingertips. The sharp, eye-wateringly strong smell of the onions was all around him, and his fingers wouldn't hold the knife properly; his hands felt awkward, the wrong shape, too soft and too weak.

Leo leaned over his shoulder and said, "Don't worry, it doesn't have to be finely diced, not for borscht."

That was probably a nice way of saying, "You're the worst onion chopper I have ever seen," but Kirk would take it. He was trying hard to ignore Leo's warm presence, the way his scent mingled with the food scents, but it was almost impossible.

"Mmm, it's been so long since I ate borscht," Leo was saying. "My grandmother used to make it as soon as the first leaves fell."

Kirk held back a growl as half an onion slipped away from his fingers, nearly bouncing off the table.

"Your grandmother who uses a spirtle," he said. He hoped the words were coming out properly.

Leo grinned. "Exactly. She's my main inspiration for cooking." He began to chop a cabbage with strokes so fast and so precise that Kirk stopped to watch. It was mesmerizing.

Chopping rhythmically, Leo said, "My mother died when I was eight, and my dad...well, he's not too good at taking care of people, and in any case he had to work. So my grandmother moved in the week after, and never moved out until she died, two years ago."

Kirk contemplated that information even as he watched Leo's fingers perform culinary magic. How did he not slice his fingers when he moved that fast?

"Sorry," Kirk said, roughly.

Leo half-turned, the knife held still. "About—? Oh, my grandmother. Thanks." His blond brows quirked, and he smiled a little. "She was so old that you're supposed to say 'Oh, it was her time', but I'm not sure that's true. She was a spitfire of an old lady. I'm sure she would have wanted to make it another twenty years, if she could."

Kirk just nodded. His 'sorry' had been for Leo's mother, as well.

He wondered about Leo's dad, who wasn't good at taking care of people. Did he appreciate his son enough? Did he see the light that burned so brightly in him?

"Are you done with the onions?" Leo asked as soon as he had expertly demolished the cabbage into thin, elegant ribbons.

Looking down at his own chopping board, covered in unevenly hacked, mangled-looking bits of onion, Kirk shrugged. "Far as I can tell?"

Leo laughed. "Good enough. Now, hmm. Would you chop the beef into smaller chunks for me?"

Kirk froze. He could already smell the meat, even though it was still wrapped and in the coolbox. If he got his hands on it in his current state...he might not be able to control himself.

When he remained silent, Leo looked over at him curiously. Then his face changed. "Wow, I'm sorry, I never asked—are you vegetarian?"

Kirk managed to turn a sudden laugh into a snort. It was tempting to say yes, just to get out of chopping beef, but that was absurd.

He had built his own smokehouse not far from the cabin, and if Leo stayed here any longer he was sure to discover it. No vegetarian would have a smokehouse, with big cuts of beef and bacon hanging from the rafters to be cured.

"No," he said shortly. "Give me the beef."

It was stupid to test himself like this, and he knew it. As soon as Leo unwrapped the package, the scent of the beef overwhelmed everything else, and he felt his mouth begin to water, his lips drawing back from his teeth.

He forced down the reaction he felt, knotting his hands into fists for a second as he struggled for control.

Leo was watching him, he could tell. He was digging into a grocery bag, pretending to ignore Kirk, but he was shooting him little glances from beneath his eyelashes.

The knife was sharp, and it sawed easily through the fresh beef. A little trickle of blood ran out, and he stared at it—then snapped himself out of that hungry stare again, with no idea how much time he had lost.

Another slice, the flesh parting under the gleaming knife. He shouldn't need a knife; he had his claws. Why cook meat, when he could just tear it apart, gulp it down—no.

He sliced the meat roughly, as if it was his own stupid pride he was dismembering, and then Leo put a hand on his arm.

"Whoa," Leo said lightly. "That's enough, we're not making steak tartare here."

Kirk breathed in deeply, remembering that he was a man.

He was not an animal, and he would not turn and grab the meat and eat it raw. He would not even tear off a portion to offer to Leo, even though all his instincts said that he should do that at this point; it was an established courting ritual for wolves. He would not give in to the wolf, not yet.

He dropped the knife. It clattered on the table.

"All done," Leo said, still in that light, cheerful voice that somehow wasn't quite natural. As though he was trying to prove something. "Let's make some soup."

Kirk hoped desperately that he wasn't scaring

Leo.

Everything felt too small, too confined—the cabin felt like a wooden box, keeping him in, enclosing him. Trapping him.

Very soon now, he would have to go. Lock himself away. Keep Leo safe.

But he couldn't leave now, while Leo was cooking for him, making him the promised borscht. He couldn't leave that last warm tie to humanity behind.

Leo had dug out the biggest frying pan, and now he was browning the meat in butter. It was another luscious, hungry-making smell, but it was less dangerous than the bloody allure of the raw beef.

Kirk sat at the table, his arms crossed over his chest, and stomped down on the urge to howl. Outside, night was falling; he could hear the squeak of bats as they left their dark hiding places to hunt.

Soon the moon would rise, one sliver away from full.

He'd never tried to resist the change this long before. Yet it should still be possible to fight it, to clamp down on the bone deep urge in his body.

He was still human, whatever his blood was trying to tell him. *But not for much longer,* said the wolf.

Leo started humming under his breath again, and the tense muscles in his shoulders were easing slowly, settling back.

A good sign; it eased a little of Kirk's own tension, too, watching him. He listened to the sweet notes in that light tenor, and watched the light-footed way Leo moved around the stove, almost as though he were dancing.

Unbidden, unwanted, the thought came: *I wish it could always be like this.*

Leo bent over and inhaled the steam rising from the large cast-iron pan. It was rich, meaty, intensely satisfying, and it brought back so many memories.

His grandmother—his Nana—had made borscht every fall, carefully selecting the best beets, the right cuts of beef. She loved cooking, and she had passed that love on to her grandson.

As far as Leo could tell, his dad Theodore thought cookery was for fools.

A man had to eat, of course, but as long as he had his meat, potatoes, and vegetables, nothing more was required. Why not eat the same meat every day, and the same vegetables too; what was wrong with that, if you ate what you liked? And it made the shopping as predictable as an algorithm table. Which, according to Theodore, was a good thing.

Leo rolled his eyes, though not without a certain fondness, as he milled pepper into the soup.

It wasn't Theodore's fault that he and Leo were so different. It was just a pity that his dad was still trying to ignore those differences, as if there was still a chance Leo would grow up into a perfect carbon copy of his dad, if only he waited long enough.

As he tasted the soup to see if it needed more pepper, he cast a quick glance at Kirk from under his eyelashes. He didn't think the big man liked being stared at, but there was something about him tonight that Leo couldn't quite place.

Kirk was always intense—Leo desperately wanted to paint those deep dark eyes under heavy brows, with their fathomless, brooding gaze, that strong implacable chin, and those wide, strong cheekbones—but tonight...tonight Kirk seemed ill at ease, restless, strangely clumsy in a way he hadn't been before.

When he walked, he moved as smoothly and silently as ever, but letting him chop onions and beef had gone so badly that Leo almost wanted to take the knife away from him, and after that Kirk had almost dropped the soup bowls twice. That wasn't like him at all.

Leo stirred the soup again, watching the strands of cabbage twist around each other. He wanted to fix whatever was wrong with Kirk, but he didn't know how. And he began to suspect that maybe he was the cause of Kirk's unease.

Maybe Kirk sensed that Leo was attracted to him.

Well, if so, at least he hasn't kicked me down the mountain yet, Leo thought with a spark of black humor.

He hummed under his breath, trying to ease his own nerves and perhaps even Kirk's.

The soup was nearly ready, and Leo began to spoon the soup into the bowls that Kirk seemed to use for everything. The borscht was a lovely deep red, like burgundy, and it smelled just right.

Leo smiled to himself. *Bite me, canned soup industry, you can't touch this.*

He put the bowls on the table, and watched with satisfaction as Kirk's eyebrows went up.

"Sour cream?" Leo asked, unconsciously falling into Kirk's habit of leaving out as many words as he could.

"Sure," Kirk said. He was looking at the soup with a strange, distracted expression—almost fearful, if that was even possible. Leo couldn't imagine anything that could scare Kirk.

Leo looked too, holding on to the tub of sour cream: was there something wrong with the food? But he could see nothing except delicious soup.

Maybe it was the color?

He looked up at Kirk from under his eyelashes, but by now Kirk's face was unreadable again.

"Dinner is served," Leo said, trying to cover the sudden awkwardness of the moment.

With a flourish, he spooned a dollop of sour cream into Kirk's bowl, where it floated like an iceberg, slowly turning pink at the edges. Then he treated himself to another spoonful and sat down, managing it first try without either falling over or dropping his crutches.

Kirk nodded to him, and they lifted their spoons without another word and began to eat.

Oh, *yes*, it was as good as it smelled.

Leo ate with relish—he'd thought he was hungry before, but it was a pale shadow to the ravening beast that seemed to have taken hold of his insides now.

Between spoonfuls, Leo watched Kirk wolf down his soup. It was incredibly satisfying to see him eat Leo's cooking, especially since he clearly was enjoying it, given the speed at which it was vanishing.

"We should really have some wine with this," Leo said thoughtfully. "But it wouldn't go well with the medicine, I suppose. Oh, and some rye bread, but I didn't think to put it on the shopping list. Maybe next time."

He said that last oh-so-carelessly, only sneaking a glance at Kirk from under his lashes when he was sure the other man wasn't looking at him. *How long are you going to let me cook for you?*

Disappointingly, Kirk merely grunted and kept eating, spoonful after spoonful disappearing in record time. He seemed to be avoiding Leo's eyes; not a good sign.

Leo's own bowl was empty sooner than he realized.

It really was very good borscht. His Nana would have approved, though she would probably have had something to say about the spices. He could hear her saying it: *Needs more pepper, my dove, to spite the devil.*

In Nana's strange, cobbled-together world of old gods and superstitions, the Devil could be kept away with black pepper, the sign of the cross, or a pebble with a hole in it that you carried on a string in your pocket. And if you didn't have any of those things, you could zap him with an old TV remote control, provided you took out the batteries first.

Seeing that Kirk's bowl was empty too, Leo looked at Kirk, but he seemed lost in some thought of his own, staring at his empty bowl as if it held the secrets of the universe.

Slowly, Leo got up again, feeling his left leg quiver under him.

It was strange that he was so tired, when he'd done practically nothing all day. It must be that he was still healing.

"Do you want some more?" he asked, shuffling over toward the stove.

When he got no reply, he turned to where Kirk was sitting at the kitchen table—and nearly fell over as one of his crutches shot away from under him.

Damn those things.

His left foot thumped down hard on the wooden floor, and the jarring, sickening pain shot all the way up his spine.

For a moment, Leo saw darkness roil in front of his eyes, and the wooden spoon in his hand clattered to the floor along with the other crutch. "Oh, damn it," he whispered, swaying on his feet and trying to blink away the blackness.

A chair scraped across the floor, and in a blur of motion, Kirk was there.

Kirk's arm was around him, and Kirk's body was pressed against him, holding him up.

So close, so warm.

He could hear Kirk's heartbeat, a deep heavy thud that resonated through his broad chest.

Leo closed his eyes and let himself have this.

The dizziness was fading already, the pain was still there but less immediate, less sickening. He would be all right in another breath...or two...

Just a moment longer, he told himself. *Just a moment and, and then I'll—*

He couldn't make himself break away. Even if

his leg would hold up, which it didn't feel like it would right now, he couldn't make himself do it.

Kirk was so warm and solid, and Leo's head rested so naturally against his shoulder. He never wanted to move again.

Leo inhaled, catching the scent of his skin beneath the soft flannel shirt. Kirk smelled good, Leo thought hazily; like woodsmoke and leather, and something else he couldn't name that seemed to belong to the woods, an earthy animalistic scent.

"T-thanks," he said, far too softly, his voice muffled in Kirk's shoulder.

But Kirk heard him.

He drew back a little—*No, don't*, Leo thought mournfully—and examined Leo, his hands grasping Leo's shoulders in a firm grip.

"You all right?" Kirk asked in that deep voice, the edges sounding even rougher now than before.

His eyes were pools to drown in. Leo stared up at him, mesmerized by that dark gaze, that rough voice, and forgot to answer him.

Kirk's big hands shook him by the shoulders,

very gently. "Leo."

"Oh," Leo said foolishly, staring up at him. "You said my name. You haven't said it since you rescued me."

Kirk blinked at him, and his face transformed again. It was that look of surprise that made him look so much younger, so much less closed down and forbidding.

Leo couldn't resist it.

He leaned into Kirk's solid warmth and locked his arms around Kirk's neck, drawing his head down with a boldness that surprised even himself.

For a moment, he felt Kirk resisting him, his muscles stiff, and Leo nearly panicked.

Then Kirk made a strange sound that sounded like a growl, and he bent his head willingly under the pressure of Leo's hands.

Their mouths met.

Leo sighed with happiness as he felt those lips against his, warm and strong. He pressed himself against Kirk, clinging, his mouth open and eager, his whole body thrumming with need.

Kirk took his mouth.

His arms were around Leo, broad fingers spread against his back, and his mouth was hot and *oh god*, it was perfect.

Leo closed his eyes, so overwhelmed that he nearly forgot to breathe, and just hung on as Kirk's mouth claimed his.

Kirk's tongue was as warm and solid as the rest of him, and Leo opened his mouth a little wider and let him in. The jolt of that entry went straight to his cock, jumping through him like the charge on a live wire.

It felt like he was melting, dissolving into Kirk's hands into a blissful puddle of heat and desire.

Eagerly, hungrily, he tilted his face up and wrapped his hands tighter around Kirk's broad shoulders, then dared to slip them into the heavy fall of Kirk's hair, freeing it from the leather tie that held it back.

Oh, that was even better than he had imagined. Sighing into Kirk's mouth, he wove his fingers through the thick strands, letting his fingertips graze Kirk's scalp.

With a half-muffled groan, Kirk arched his

back, pressing his head into Leo's hands like a cat being stroked.

They clung together tightly, mouths sealed together, and then Kirk's hands slid down his spine and cupped his ass.

Leo gasped into Kirk's mouth. *Oh god, yes, do that, hold me there, oh—*

Kirk's broad hands were so warm, and they cupped his ass so firmly, and all Leo wanted was more. Anything, everything.

Rip my clothes off and bend me over the kitchen table, do it, do it, he chanted in his head, not quite brave enough to say it out loud, not yet, though he felt reckless and dizzy, almost drunk with desire.

He licked at the inside of Kirk's mouth, feeling the other man shudder under his hands.

Please. Anything you want. Please.

Kirk made another low growling sound that seemed to reverberate through the floorboards, and pulled Leo tighter against his body.

Leo felt his feet leave the floor. Kirk was holding him up completely now, with Leo's back against the wall next to the stove. It didn't seem to cost Kirk any effort at all to hold him like this, and it reminded Leo of Kirk carrying him down the mountain with huge loping strides, as confident and sure-footed as a mountain cat.

God, how that strength turned him on.

Kirk's head was bent down to Leo's, claiming his mouth with fierce and fiery kisses again and again.

Leo closed his eyes and lost himself in the singing of his body.

Without conscious thought, he spread his legs around the width of Kirk's thighs, drawing him in closer.

Then Leo knocked his left leg against the stove, just as he was trying to wrap it around Kirk's thigh.

A bolt of agony shot through him, and he yelped in pain.

With a wrench that made Leo ache inside, Kirk tore his mouth away. His breath whooshed out in a great rush, and then he pressed his forehead against Leo's.

Abruptly, Leo felt himself sliding down the wall.

Kirk was letting him go, moving away, his face dark and unreadable—no, *no!* This was all wrong!

His leg throbbed as though it was on fire, and he couldn't get up. He sat there, legs spread, his back against the wall, and stretched out a hand as if that was enough to keep Kirk close.

"Don't stop," Leo said, his voice a croak. "I just —my leg hit the stove, it's nothing—"

Kirk was out of his reach now.

He was bent over the kitchen table, his strong hands clutching the wooden edge, and he breathed in long, deep, shaking breaths. His black hair fell forward, and Leo couldn't see his face.

"Need to go," Kirk said then, in a voice so deep and rough that Leo had to strain to understand him. "I —"

He paused, breathing hard, and Leo felt his own heartbeat accelerate into near-panic. What was wrong, what *was* this?

Kirk breathed in deeply. "Hunting trip," he

said, as if the words were being torn from his throat.

Leo simply stared at him. He couldn't process this at all. He wanted desperately to see Kirk's face, to understand why his voice had broken into this gravelly roar.

His hands clenching into fists, Kirk straightened up.

"I need to go," he said carefully, slowly, as if the words were coming with some immense, unguessable effort. "Tonight. Hunting trip. Not your fault."

"Not my fault?" Leo said, his own voice shaking. "Kirk, I'm sorry, if I…I took things too fast, please don't go—"

"Have to," Kirk said, and now his eyes were finally meeting Leo's.

Leo gasped with surprise and shock at what he saw there.

Kirk's eyes were burning, his mouth a thin grim line. He looked like he was being torn apart by a weight of pain and grief that Leo couldn't understand, though he felt the shock of that gaze stab at his heart.

"Stay here," Kirk said then. "Back in a couple days."

"You still—you want me to stay?" Leo asked, helplessly trying to scrabble back up the wall, to grab hold of Kirk and stop him somehow.

To his surprise Kirk bent over him and lifted him up again—lifted him up all the way, cradling him to his chest.

"You are welcome here," Kirk said, very roughly, enunciating the words with great care. "Always."

Leo tried to tilt his head back enough to meet Kirk's eyes, but Kirk was looking away from him, his face hidden again behind a curtain of dark curly hair, his jaw set in a hard line.

Kirk deposited him on one of the kitchen chairs, setting him down carefully but firmly. Then he turned away with surprising speed and grabbed the old army rucksack that lay by the door.

"Wait—" Leo called, but all he heard was the creak and thud of the screen door opening, then slamming shut. When he made his limping way to the front door, Kirk was already gone.

Kirk's breath echoed in his ears. In the deep quiet of the woods at night, it seemed very loud. But not loud enough to cover the other sounds, the ones that receded behind him as he ran up the mountain path.

Leo's heartbeat: too fast at first, then slowing as he recovered from the shock of Kirk's departure.

Leo's ragged breathing, and the scrape of his crutches on the kitchen floor.

A curse, barely audible, in that sweet tenor voice.

Kirk was running away from the cabin, running upwind, and yet he still thought he could catch Leo's scent, with its new overtones of worry and shock.

It took everything Kirk had to keep moving.

Every instinct he possessed was screaming at him to go back, to finish what he had started.

To claim his mate.

But that was wrong. Even if Leo wanted him—something he could still barely believe was possible, and yet Leo had kissed him and sunk his hands into Kirk's hair, and the scent of his excitement was as unmistakable as it was startling—even if Leo wanted him for just that moment, he was not Kirk's to take. To despoil.

Leo didn't know what was at stake.

To be fair, neither did Kirk. Not really. Not from experience, anyway.

Before he had been made into a monster, Kirk hadn't known such a thing existed. Desperate for some way to rid himself of the change, he'd tried to find information on werewolves, but there was nothing. Fairy tales and superstitions and silly movies, nothing real.

Then he'd started reading up on wolves, on wolf behavior. The stark sentences had struck him to the heart: *wolves mate for life.*

For him, that might even have been true before the change. His few attempts at casual sex had never been fulfilling, and he never understood why men were supposed to love one-night stands. It seemed tawdry to him: mere rutting, as desperate as it was unsatisfying. He never wanted to look his partners in the face, much less speak to them afterwards, and he would slink away in the early morning, ashamed of himself.

Then he'd joined the Army, and they'd singled him out and made him into a monster.

After that, Kirk believed that nobody would ever want him again, and had arranged his life to suit himself.

Now...now all his certainties were suddenly shaking loose.

It wasn't possible, his rational mind was telling him. Leo might like the man, but that didn't mean he could love the wolf.

And for better or for worse, Kirk *was* the wolf.

The wolf was him.

The beast reared up in him now, howling to get out. He could feel his clothes itching, the backpack a strange and annoying weight against his spine. Running felt wrong: why wasn't he on all fours?

Moving faster, Kirk hoped desperately that he

would make it to the old hunting lodge in time. It was his only refuge during the change: an old, dilapidated shack, so high up the mountain, so inaccessible, that he could weather the change there if he had to, without fearing that someone would find him.

Up until now, it hadn't been necessary; he had always let the wolf run free, roaming through the woods. In hunting season, he took care to drive to a remote area where no hunters ever came, before letting the change come over him.

But Kirk had made contingency plans, just in case, and now those plans would save Leo from being mauled.

His backpack held a change of clothes, some dried food and water, the chain with its heavy snap lock, and the collar.

If he changed too early, if the wolf took over, the backpack would be lost in the woods, and he would have no way to restrain himself...*no*. He couldn't allow that to happen. Leo wouldn't be safe. The wolf would double back and take him.

Snarling under his breath, he ran faster, finding his way effortlessly in the faint starlight.

Everything was tinted gray, but he could see

clearly and hear every noise for miles around. Many scents were on the wind, but nothing that would stop him; no other humans. If he could still call himself that.

He'd been running for at least an hour, at his fastest speed.

He was close.

But so was the wolf.

There was no path up to the hunting lodge, and the going was rough and uncertain, but Kirk's feet found the way effortlessly. He bounded over a slope of scree, sharp rocks and debris left behind after an old earth slide.

Very close now.

He could smell his own scent markers, left behind during the previous change. There were no other markers; no wolves ever came here, or even approached his territory, perhaps because his scent warned them away.

The slope grew steeper, and his breath sounded harsher now, the pad of his feet more forceful.

Up ahead, against a rocky ridge, he could see the dun-colored walls of the shack.

Behind him, the moon was rising. He felt it like a physical presence looming over him.

Close, so close.

Three more lunging steps, and the door of the shack was in front of him. It was locked, and his fingers fumbled for the key.

The door creaked open, and Kirk exhaled for a long breath, feeling a measure of relief.

Sanctuary. But he still wasn't safe, not yet.

Slamming the door shut behind him, he threw the backpack onto the floor, then yanked off his clothes and boots as quickly as possible. There was no point in waiting for the wolf to shred them.

Naked, he felt bristles prickle beneath his skin, and cursed under his breath.

The change was coming.

He still had to chain himself up, or all of this would be for nothing. There was no point in even locking the shack's front door again: a simple wooden door would never hold the wolf.

The back wall of the lodge would.

The lodge was built into the mountain ridge it stood on, and the back wall was pure bedrock. Long ago, whoever first owned the lodge had sunk a couple of steel spikes into it, driven deep into the rock, with heavy rings hanging off the end. For what purpose, Kirk couldn't guess—a gun rack? something to do with mountaineering?—but he was grateful.

He had tested the strength of those rings, and he knew he couldn't break them. Nor could he draw the spike back out of the rock with his bare hands.

Moving as fast as he could, he looped the heavy chain through one of the rings, and then attached the collar with the snap lock.

It looked strange when he was done; vaguely obscene, as though he was building his own private bondage dungeon. *Ha.* His mouth twisted bitterly. *If only this was for pleasure.*

The chain links chinked against each other, a loud metallic sound that made him want to snap his ears back.

He wrestled the leather collar around his throat and closed it, tugging hard upon the strap to secure it. It felt thick and heavy and strange.

Finally he was done. The chain was short, and

he couldn't move more than a few steps away from the bedrock wall.

Kirk knelt naked on the wooden floor, his back against the cold rock, and waited for the change to consume him.

Leo was so mad he wanted to throw dishes at the wall. He wanted to wreck something, preferably something that belonged to Kirk.

In Leo's family, when you were mad, you did everything you could to hide it, or you used cold sarcasm to express it. Anything else was a weakness.

Well, fuck that, Leo thought, looking around the kitchen for something he could destroy.

His eye fell on the two blue earthenware bowls, the ones they'd been eating soup out of.

He picked one up...and then he paused.

It was a lovely bowl, with a midnight blue glaze that melted into a softer blue at the top, and it looked old. In his mind's eye, he saw Kirk's big, rough hands handling those bowls so very carefully, as if to compensate for the strange clumsiness that didn't belong to a man who could move so swiftly and silently, like a big hunting cat.

"Damn it," Leo whispered, and he put the bowl back down.

Damn *Kirk.*

Why would Kirk even do this? *Talk about things that make no sense.*

Leo had thought about different scenarios, about what might happen when the spark between Kirk and himself started to blaze up into a bonfire.

In all his wildest dreams, he hadn't imagined that Kirk would kiss him back—oh god, those *kisses*, it was as though he could still feel the fierce press of Kirk's mouth on his—and then run away as though his life depended on it.

Kirk seemed like the last person in the world who would run away from a confrontation.

Oh, but he was going on a hunting trip, *sure.*

Leo made a wry face, thinking about that.

Kirk had gone out hunting in the middle of the night, in pitch dark, on foot. And as far as Leo could tell, without a gun. That backpack he'd grabbed wasn't big enough to conceal a hunting rifle, or even a bow and arrows.

Somehow Kirk seemed more the type to use a bow and arrows; Leo couldn't even say why, except that it seemed to fit him. There was something primitive about him.

Leo picked up his crutches and awkwardly shuffled into the cabin's small living room. His leg was feeling much better, and it was an effort to keep the weight off it. He wanted to throw the crutches out and start walking again.

He wanted to go after Kirk.

Leo shook his head at himself. *Don't be crazy.*

Kirk knew this area; he didn't. He had no business going out at night, not with his leg all busted up.

Even though it was dark, Kirk would be all right. Leo would only come to grief if he came out after him.

Besides, what sort of message was that going to send?

If you kiss a guy and he runs away from you, that's not a clue to go chasing after him. Who do you think you are, Pepe le Pew?

That was the kind of common sense he needed here; the kind of thing his Nana would have said.

Leo sighed and let himself drop into one of the old armchairs near the fireplace. The furniture was simple and old, but comfortable: two armchairs, a small couch covered in a striped Navajo blanket, the fireplace, and some shelves of books and knick-knacks.

The fire was very low, little more than glowing embers.

It fit Leo's mood.

He wanted to turn back time and flash back to when he was happily cooking breakfast for Kirk, maybe sneaking a glance or two at the broad swell of his shoulders when the other man looked away.

But noooo, you had to push it. Goddamn it.

By now, Leo wasn't sure if he was madder at Kirk or himself.

He imagined himself sitting in a coffee bar with Cherie, his best friend from art school, and telling her, "I went on a hiking trip to figure out my life, and instead I found this *amazing* guy. And we kissed."

He could just picture Cherie leaning forward,

her long earrings dangling while she grinned her big gap-toothed grin at him. "That's great! Tell me more!"

"Well, and then he ran off into the night claiming he had to go hunting. After buying a ton of food at the grocery store, even. *And* he wasn't carrying a gun."

"Riiiiight. So, after you scared him away, then what?"

That was the question.

Leo stared into the glowing embers.

He could go to bed. It was late.

Get up in the morning, cook breakfast, wait for Kirk to come back...

It felt wrong.

Or I could look for the keys to his truck, drive down to town, get a hotel.

That wasn't right, either.

Crazy as it was, he felt deep down in his bones that he should stay here. Or maybe that wasn't entirely it, either. He didn't want to stay here, he didn't want to leave.

What it came down to was this: he didn't want to leave Kirk alone.

Restless, he got up again, dragging the crutches up under his arms, and went to stare out of the open shutters.

It was so dark outside. The moon was up now, but he could still barely see a thing.

Did Kirk have a flashlight? Where was he even going? Was he planning to sleep out in the open? It was cold out, probably only just above freezing.

It didn't make any sense. If he'd taken the truck, Leo would have assumed that Kirk was driving out to some bar to get hammered.

But walking out in the dead of night, on foot…that seemed much more serious somehow. Much more dangerous.

Damn him.

Leo was never going to get any sleep, not tonight. Now that the anger was dying away, worry was taking its place, and it was making him crazy.

Leo limped away from the window, moving slowly toward the shelf of books and knick-knacks.

Maybe he could find something here that would tell him more about Kirk.

Something that would give him a clue how a perfect kiss could go so very, very wrong.

Kirk yanked at the chain again, his paws scrabbling to get hold of the slippery metal.

The chain had man-scent on it, not just Kirk's but others', faint and old.

Hardware store, that faint annoying presence at the back of his mind supplied, but the words didn't mean anything.

The chain was *wrong*, it was in his way, he wanted it *gone*. The sound it made as it clanked against the wall hurt his ears.

But even as he felt his spine crackle with effort, the chain held fast.

It was tied to something around his neck, something that smelled of cow. Old, dead cow-skin.

He tried to get his claws under it and rip it off, again and again, without success.

Outside this den of stone, the moon was up.

He could feel it pulling at him.

It was time to hunt. The night was alive with sounds and scents.

Bats squeaked as they flitted and circled under the clouds, calling their hunting-cry for those with ears to hear. Birds called warnings and come-hithers and stay-aways. Leaves fell, hitting the ground with soft thuds. A squirrel gnawed at a nut, safely hidden inside a tree.

Kirk threw back his head and howled.

It was a good howl, a strong howl, but this place was too enclosed, and the sound rang off the walls instead of fading into the distance.

He howled again, louder.

There was no answering call. There never was; the part of him that could remember things knew that he had never heard another wolf call back to him.

Yet somehow, he felt that this time, there should be a reply.

His mate should be calling for him.

He was too far away from the home-den, he couldn't find the scent of his mate in the air anymore, and that was wrong too.

Faint reminders of him lingered on Kirk's paws, on his muzzle.

Not your mate, said the other him, but that made no sense either.

Leo. His mate's name was Leo, and his mate was his. Nobody else's.

Kirk needed to mark him, cover him with his own scent inside and out, so nobody else would dare to even approach him. He would fight anyone who tried.

He yanked at the chain again, trying to make it give.

It rattled and clanked, but it didn't move.

Kirk howled again, a long rip of sound that split the air into fragments around him.

I am here. I am here. Where are you?

Leo was probably doing something crazy. But he wasn't going to let that stop him.

All his hiking gear was going to come in handy at last—the GPS, the headlamp with the bright LED bulbs, the heavy boots, the collapsible walking poles, and the rescue blanket.

Don't let me need to use the rescue blanket. Please.

Leo dropped the crutches by the couch. He couldn't use them on the rocky terrain; he would use his walking poles instead. That meant putting more weight on his injured leg, but he thought he should be able to handle it by now. And if not, well, he had painkillers. Though he'd rather save them in case Kirk needed them.

That was the problem with this whole situation: he simply couldn't believe that Kirk might be in need of rescue, but he couldn't take the chance that he was wrong.

Besides, it was only fair that Leo got to rescue

him, this time around.

It just didn't feel right. Kirk lived here, and had apparently lived here all his life, if Dr Ogilvy was to be believed. He knew this area. He was strong as a bear, or even stronger, and he walked as surefootedly as a cat.

But all the same, Leo couldn't stop thinking about all the things that could go wrong.

His mind and his gut were on opposing sides: his gut said, *Kirk will be okay.* But his mind wouldn't stop throwing up nightmare scenarios. Kirk lost, Kirk alone, Kirk hurting.

Like Leo was, before Kirk saved his life.

Leo was still undecided when he heard the wolf howling. That tore it.

It was a sound Leo had heard before while hiking, but never this close, this loud.

It sounded horrible, a ragged wail of hunger and aggression.

It came again and again, and he had no idea if it was one wolf or a whole pack of them.

And Kirk was out there in the darkness, alone!

Leo checked over his supplies one last time, then girded on his backpack. It was much lighter than before; he'd dropped all the stuff he didn't need, like the tent and the stupid lightweight stove, but he'd kept all the emergency gear, the sleeping bag, and the honey-nut bars and water.

As he stepped out the door of the cabin and switched on his headlamp, spilling bright white light into the dark forest, Leo hoped desperately that he wasn't about to go on a fool's errand.

After all, he could be wrong about where Kirk was going.

Again, his mind was saying one thing; his gut another. His mind said, *Kirk could be anywhere.* His gut said: *he's there, where the cross mark is.*

The cross was the only thing he had to go on.

As soon as Leo found the old map in a dusty frame, hanging near the cabin's front door, he knew this was the clue he'd been hunting for.

It was a topographical map, and it showed the criss-crossing dirt roads around the town and all the mountain ridges and peaks in vertiginous detail. And someone had scrawled a little black cross on it, right where the cabin was, and another little black cross some distance away. There was a little black dot there too, indicating a small building of some sort.

Judging by the contours on the map, it was a steep climb. It was going to be tough on his leg, and Dr Ogilvy was probably going to raise hell.

Leo didn't care.

He hoisted the backpack higher on his shoulders and left the cabin, stepping out into the dark.

Kirk howled again and again, until his throat began to feel raw. He'd been howling for a long time, but hours meant nothing to him now.

Still no response.

Not even from his mate.

Where *was* he? Why wasn't he coming?

The cow-skin thing around his throat hurt now, rubbing against his skin, but he couldn't stop pulling at it, trying to get it away from him.

Outside, the birds were changing their song.

In all their various trills and calls, they were saying, *Sun is coming. Day is coming, day is coming.* He couldn't understand all the stupid things birds said to each other, and he didn't want to, but the big things were easy enough.

His paws were getting tired of scrabbling on the floor, tearing uselessly at the chinking metal chain.

He was getting tired all over.

His skin hurt.

Sun was coming. Day was coming.

That meant something else was coming, too. *The hurting.*

And after the hurting, he would be different.

Weak. Furless, clawless. Like a newborn pup.

Kirk put his head down on his tired paws and whined, low in his throat. He was so tired, and thirsty, and hungry. His stomach was empty, and his throat was raw with the pain of the thing around his neck.

Then, several miles off, a blackbird gave the clear, high whistle that was its warning call.

Something was coming up the ridge, something that wasn't the sun.

Something *big*. A two-leg.

He tore at the chain again, making it clatter. It still wouldn't give.

Growling, he waited for whatever was approaching.

If it came to challenge him, he would tear out its throat and feast upon its blood.

Leo cursed in a steady stream as he clambered up the steep ridge. Then he had to stop, because his lungs were giving out on him.

He paused, bent over, hands on his knees, and tried to catch his breath.

His leg ached fiercely. He'd been walking for hours, taking it slow, careful not to get lost or stress his leg too much. He'd already taken one pain killer, but it must be wearing off. He had more, but he wanted to save them in case Kirk needed them.

At least he had some idea that he was on the right trail. Even though there barely *was* a trail. If he didn't have the old topo-map, with its precise contours of every single bit of the terrain, as well as the GPS, he would have been hopelessly lost.

Far above his head, on top of the ridge, something loomed that didn't look like a rock formation. Too square, too dark against the gray and brown shades of the ridge.

He couldn't see the dark shape now; the steep incline hid it from view. But its location matched the little scrawled X on the map exactly.

The air was cold up here, but the stars above his head were amazing. They were so bright, and the moon was, too, though it was nearing the horizon by now. His little headlamp only gave a small beam of light; it helped to illuminate the path right in front of his feet, but the surroundings stayed dark.

Leo straightened up and began to climb again, following the barely visible trail as it wound from switchback to switchback, slowly crawling up the ridge. As long as he kept going up, he knew he was doing okay.

He kept trying to put more weight on his unhurt right leg, but even though the hiking poles helped, he still had to use his left leg to balance himself and keep moving in a straight line. He couldn't limp all the way up to the ridge.

Still, he could deal with that. His leg wasn't broken, and he didn't think he was doing irreparable damage to it. It just *hurt*.

He clamped his teeth together and kept going. *I can do this.*

Another wolf howl came out of the darkness, and Leo froze.

It sounded so close. Was it just the stillness of the night, amplifying the sound? Or was there really a wolf, close by?

He'd never seen a wolf. From what he could remember, wolves weren't supposed to be dangerous unless they were rabid, or unless you were unlucky enough to encounter a whole pack, or a mother with cubs.

One wolf by itself wasn't supposed to be a danger, not to a man.

I hope someone told the wolf that.

He kept climbing. The going was slow and painful, but he was still making progress. He wasn't going to give up now.

The next switchback leveled out, and when he craned his neck back, trying to get the headlamp's light on the rock wall, there was no wall.

He was on the top of the ridge.

He looked around, swiveling his head left and right, and yes! *There.* That was the dark shape he had spotted earlier. It was easier to see, now that the sky to the east was slowly growing lighter.

A shed built into the rock, dark and squat. There was no light from the one small window.

Dead on target.

Now he had to find out if Kirk was hiding there, or if this whole exhausting journey had been for nothing.

Kirk shook his head, making the chain clatter. His skin itched, and he could feel the moon's pull getting weaker, and that annoying other-self in his head getting stronger.

His senses were in turmoil.

Leo's scent was on the wind.

That makes no sense, the irritating voice in the back of his mind kept telling him. *Leo isn't here.*

Leo *couldn't* be here. He was safe, he was home, he was nowhere near the hunting lodge.

The hurting was coming, and it was confusing everything. He couldn't tell sounds apart anymore.

Was that Leo's heartbeat he heard, or his own?

A door creaked, and then light hurt his eyes.

Not the sun, not yet.

Or was it? A small sun?

No. A lamp.

Kirk squinted, trying to see against the sudden fierce whiteness that played over his fur, shining into his eyes.

The scent of the intruder was overwhelming, and he couldn't ignore his own nose any longer.

Leo.

He flattened his ears, scrabbling desperately back into the wall, whining when it wouldn't give way.

Leo couldn't be here. That was *wrong*.

Kirk wasn't even sure why it was wrong—Leo was his mate, Leo *should* be here—but now, for the first time ever, it was the annoying voice in the back of his mind that was howling. The voice of the furless one, the two-leg, not the wolf. The two-leg was desperate to hide himself, but the wolf had no idea why.

"Oh crap, was that you I heard howling?" Leo's voice said, overlaid with the scent of fear and confusion and something else: pity? His voice sounded strange, full of buzzing and burring undertones that only the wolf could hear. "Hey, take it easy, don't hurt yourself."

That was all wrong, too. Kirk wasn't hurt. Kirk wasn't going to be hurt. It was Leo who would be hurt if he came closer.

But that made no sense, why would Kirk hurt Leo? All he wanted to do was mount him, claim him, mark him with scent and seed. That was *right*.

He whined, low in his throat, confused and hungry for the scent and sound of his mate.

Then Leo stepped closer. "God, I can't believe someone would chain an animal up like this in the middle of nowhere," he said. His breathing was fast and high in his throat, nervous. "You poor thing. You're bleeding."

Kirk sniffed the air. Yes, there was blood in it; his own blood, crisp and metallic, from the pain-thing around his neck.

Not important. Not important at all. He would heal. Didn't Leo know that he would heal?

"Let me see if I—" Leo was saying, his hands reaching out toward Kirk. "Please don't bite, I just want to get that collar off—"

He still smelled of fear, but Kirk could read the determination in the set of his chin. So brave, his mate.

In the distance, Kirk could hear a chorus of birdsong, bright with hope for a new day.

Dawn was here.

He keened, curling in upon himself despite the vicious tug of the pain-thing around his neck.

His paws hurt, and his skin felt like it was tearing apart.

He was changing.

Not now, the voice in his head yelled at him. *Now now, not here, not in front of Leo! Run!*

But there was nowhere to hide, and he couldn't run.

He could only moan in pain as the change swept over him.

Leo stepped back, his eyes wide, pupils dilating. "What—what are you—" he said, his voice raw with surprise and shock.

Kirk couldn't answer, even if he knew how. The pain clawed him open. It was turning him inside out, remaking him, pulling apart flesh and bone into new shapes.

Closing his stinging eyes, he howled for the last time.

Then he let the blackness take him.

Leo drew in a shaking breath. His legs felt rubbery, and it wasn't just from the effort of the climb up the ridge.

What was *happening*?

He thought he had a handle on this when he came in: someone had chained up this poor dog, letting the collar rub its neck so raw it was bleeding and howling.

The dog was huge, bigger than any dog he had ever seen, with a lush black pelt and luminous green eyes. Its teeth were big and white, and its eyes rolled in its head as it tried to scramble away from Leo.

Maybe it would be more sensible to leave the dog alone, but Leo couldn't stand to see an animal in pain. The sound of its howling chilled his bones.

He wanted to help. He still needed to look for Kirk, but he couldn't just leave this poor dog chained up like this.

But now—now something was happening that he couldn't understand at all.

The light from his headlamp careened over the walls of the old shack, throwing sharp and spiky shadows. The dark rock, the gleaming chain links, and the huge black dog all looked like something out of a nightmare.

The dog was curling in upon itself, whining low in its throat, an awful sound.

Leo was close enough to touch it, but some instinct made him back off.

The dog wasn't just in pain, it was *changing*.

Its fur slowly melted away, until Leo could see the skin beneath. Its huge paws were changing color, and they seemed to be growing longer, thinner.

Leo breathed in fast, shocky breaths. He couldn't tear himself away from this bizarre spectacle, though his instincts were screaming at him to *run*, run far away and hide.

Now the dog's whole shape was changing: the spine, the head. More fur disappeared, leaving naked pink skin behind. The tail shortened, then disappeared altogether.

Leo stared at the creature, and he felt the hair lift on the back of his neck.

It wasn't a dog any longer. It was—it was becoming *human*.

Leo staggered back a step, leaning heavily upon his walking poles. This was unbelievable. This was—this couldn't be happening.

But it was. The light from his headlamp was cold and white, and it showed everything all too clearly: the way the dog's ears were slowly growing rounder and losing the tufts of fur, the way its narrow, furry thighs thickened into naked, muscular human legs.

"Oh god," Leo breathed, not sure if it was a prayer or a plea for help.

He watched the dog's elongated snout recede back into a different shape.

A human shape.

A strangely familiar shape.

Leo felt his heartbeat stutter.

He shivered all over, cold with fear and shock, as he watched the dog's features slowly transform into those of a man.

A man with dark eyes, a strong jaw, a chin you could use for a chisel...

Even twisted in pain, that face was unmistakable. Leo had been staring at those dark, deep-set eyes for days now, trying to memorize them so he could paint them some day.

No. *No.*

This can't be real. I'm dreaming.

Leo stepped forward and awkwardly knelt by the creature's side, dropping the walking poles on the wooden floor.

His voice shaking, he whispered, "Kirk?"

Kirk groaned in pain as the change swept over him. It was slow, so slow and painful, and above all: incomplete.

The wolf's blood still ran hot in him.

He could feel it coursing through his veins, inflaming him with the wolf's simple, urgent needs. It would only recede a little in the coming hours, then return with a vengeance for tonight's full moon.

Hazily, he tried to remember what he was supposed to be doing. He should at least eat and drink something during the day, maybe wash away the blood congealing on his neck...

He sniffed the air, and his eyes snapped open.

It was *not* a dream, or a fantasy conjured up by his mating instincts.

It was real.

Leo was here.

His scent crashed over Kirk like a ten-foot tsunami. He reeled, his head spinning with *want-need-touch.*

Leo was *here*, he was close enough to touch, and his hands were...what was he doing?

He was taking off the collar.

Oh, sweet freedom. Kirk surged forward, his paws—hands—barely obeying him, his jaw dropping as he tried to somehow swallow Leo's scent and make it a part of him.

He crashed into Leo headfirst, bearing him down against the floor.

"Hey, hey, whoa, it's me," Leo was saying. The collar dropped from his hands, forgotten.

Kirk could barely understand him. Words were so futile, so flat, compared to the spectrum of scents that Leo was putting out. Leo was worried, concerned, a little afraid, but underneath it all was a warmth that Kirk felt in the pit of his own belly.

That warmth was for *him*.

He licked a long stripe from the just-visible tip of Leo's collarbone to his ear, tasting him, losing himself in the symphony of taste and scent.

"Okay, this is getting too weird for me," Leo said, his voice stuttering a little. "Kirk? Do you know where you are? What happened to you? Who—who chained you up like this?"

Kirk felt his voice, hearing it resonate against his breastbone.

He ignored the words. What mattered was the warm tone of Leo's voice, the slick caress of his tongue against his palate as he made sounds, and the scents that rose off him in intoxicating waves.

He growled a little, happily, and pawed at Leo's clothes. They were in the way, covering up the most important parts of him. If only he still had his claws, he could just rip them, but his stupid nails were too fragile.

The jeans were especially difficult. He poked at them, feeling the shape of the metal buttons, and tried to remember how they came off.

Then, frustrated, he bent his head and just licked at Leo's crotch. It tasted mostly like fabric and dye, but there was a hint of Leo's scent there as well.

"Oh *god*," Leo half-whispered, trembling. The

soft bulge of his cock twitched under Kirk's tongue, growing bigger under the heavy denim. "Kirk, say something, okay? Tell me—"

Words. Leo wanted words from him.

Kirk scraped them from his throat. "Leo," he rasped.

The effect was immediate. The citrusy edge of fear in Leo's scent mellowed into warm amber, and the shocked expression in his eyes grew soft.

"Oh, thank goodness. You're here. I'm so glad I found you. Are you okay? Let me—"

So many words. Not at all necessary.

Demonstratively, Kirk licked another stripe up Leo's crotch, lingering at the place where the seams met. The fabric was growing darker there, wet from his tongue.

"Um," Leo said, then groaned helplessly as Kirk dug insistently with sharp jabs of his tongue, probing at the seams.

Kirk could smell Leo's arousal as clearly as his own. Who needed *words* when they had this?

The wolf was overpowering him again,

growling in his ears, telling him to claim his mate now, now, *now*.

Leo's slim fingers ghosted over his neck, slipping down to his shoulders in a tentative caress.

Kirk basked in his touch. Strangely, Leo wasn't afraid of him. He wasn't repulsed by Kirk. Not by his change, nor by the wolf that still lived in him and would always be a part of him.

It was a miracle, but it was true. Kirk could smell it. There was no fear left in Leo's scent, only uncertainty mixed with a growing musk of arousal.

Fumbling, Kirk's clumsy, wrong-shaped fingers found the zipper to Leo's coat. He pulled at it, dimly remembering how to ease it down so it didn't break. He'd broken plenty of zippers in times like these.

There, that was one less layer between him and Leo.

So many layers left, though: wool sweater, t-shirt, jeans, underwear, socks, hiking boots.

Silly furless humans, said the wolf, his scent-images so clear that Kirk could easily supply the words. *Always covering themselves up.*

Kirk agreed. His own fur was mostly gone, now, but he still felt warm, his blood running hot with the wolf's more-than-human heat.

He wanted to share that warmth with Leo.

Leo was helping, now, pulling the wool sweater over his own head with shaking hands. "If you want this, I—if you're sure—" he was saying, his voice as shaky as his hands.

Kirk grunted. There was no room for doubt, not with the wolf's absolute certainty howling in his brain. He knew what he wanted.

He dug underneath the t-shirt, finding delicious bare skin there to touch and taste. His hands strayed upward, stroking and exploring, until they encountered the little nubs of Leo's nipples. So soft under his fingers, though they tightened up as soon as he rubbed them.

Leo moaned softly, and the sound was like sweet honey.

Let me hear what other sounds you can make.

Leo was losing track of what was happening. It was all going so fast that it felt like a dream.

An incredibly vivid, incredibly sexy, unbelievably bizarre dream.

Kirk—who had been an *animal* not ten minutes ago—Kirk was naked, aroused, and rubbing up against him, his hands pushing Leo's t-shirt up.

He was a little uncoordinated, his fingers fumbling with the cotton hem, then sliding down Leo's chest again.

Can't really blame him for that, Leo thought giddily. *He had* paws *ten minutes ago. And now he's—oh god—licking my stomach.*

He pulled the t-shirt over his head, shivering as the cold air hit his bare skin. His nipples perked up, and now they felt even more sensitive than before.

The headlamp pulled off his head along with the t-shirt, ruffling up his hair. He left the lamp where it was, shining brightly through the t-shirt's thin fabric. It made the light a little softer, a little warmer. And he did want the light; he wanted to see Kirk.

He wanted to convince himself that this was real. He'd never had a dream this crazy, and it certainly *felt* real...almost to good to be real.

Looking down, he sucked in a breath, feeling heat curl in his belly.

There was a *lot* of Kirk, even when he was sitting down with his legs folded up under him, and Leo had a spectacular view of Kirk's naked back and his broad shoulders. His hair was loose, and Leo slipped his fingers into the wild tangle of curls, stroking the nape of Kirk's neck.

Kirk responded by licking him again, and Leo moaned out loud, arching up against the rough rasp of Kirk's tongue.

Low in his throat, Kirk made a sound that was close to a growl. It sounded very much like the noises he had made in the kitchen, trying desperately to speak.

That makes a little more sense now, Leo thought; *he must have been suffering the effects of the...the other him. That's why he ran from me.* That distracted him for a moment from what Kirk was doing, and he winced at a sudden stab of sympathy. *And then...then he hid himself here.*

The conclusion was inescapable. Kirk had run to this refuge, and locked himself away. Chained himself up, before the change began. Kirk had known this was going to happen.

Leo shivered.

It was very hard to think while Kirk's hands were drawing warm patterns on his stomach.

What if this was just adrenaline-fueled desperation? What if Kirk changed his mind again, after...after this?

God, that would kill me. He sucked in a deep breath and set his jaw. *Still, I'll take it. I'm not going to be the one to run away.*

Kirk was licking broad, wet stripes up his stomach, and the change from warm tongue to cold night air was making him shiver deliciously.

Leo sank his hands deeper into Kirk's hair, oddly reassured by the strong bone of his skull. *Whatever happens later,* he thought, *I get to have this. I get to have* you.

Kirk couldn't get enough of tasting Leo. His skin tasted the way he smelled, and it was intoxicating.

When he dipped his tongue into the sweet dimple of Leo's navel, Leo's hands tugged at his hair and he made a tiny sound, just a huff of breath.

In the half-dark, broken only by the muted light of Leo's headlamp, Kirk could see everything as clear as day.

He could see Leo's dilated pupils, so dark and hungry. He could see the signs of arousal in the trembling muscles of his stomach, the way his lips parted, and the way his chest rose and fell with his fast and shallow breathing.

How he wanted to taste that mouth, but he wasn't willing to give up his current goal: the path down Leo's stomach, with its trail of little blond hairs leading down to the hardness he could feel bulging below.

His fingers kept slipping off the buttons of the

damned jeans. The hiking boots and socks had been easier to remove, knots and all, than these jeans with their cursed buttons that fit so tightly, constraining the heat of Leo's arousal beneath.

He had to concentrate. He couldn't rip Leo's jeans off with his teeth...well. He probably could, but Leo might not appreciate it.

By using every last remnant of focus he had, he managed to undo the metal buttons one by one.

As soon as each button slipped free, he bent to press a kiss against the soft cotton below. Leo moaned when he did it, very softly.

Between buttons, he skimmed his hands up Leo's sides, enjoying the little sounds he made. So Leo was ticklish, was he?

The last button slipped free.

He tugged the jeans down Leo's slimly muscled thighs.

Ahhh. The scent of his arousal was much stronger now, salt and musk, and Kirk inhaled deeply, burying his face in Leo's white cotton underwear.

"What are you—oh," Leo said, his hands

grazing Kirk's scalp. "*Oh…*"

He was so responsive, so sweet, so willing.

Kirk lifted him up easily, sliding both hands under the delicious curve of his ass, and then tugging down his underwear with one hand. He didn't *need* to do it like that, a part of himself acknowledged—but he didn't miss Leo's soft gasp as he felt himself being lifted into the air.

He likes my strength. It was an amazing, heady feeling. *He likes it still, even now he knows what I am. He wants me still.*

There was no pity or repulsion or morbid curiosity in Leo's wide-open eyes, or in the drifting, complex layers of his scent. He was guileless, open, wanting. Wanting him.

Rubbing his face against the soft bare skin of Leo's stomach, he licked and sucked his way back down again.

Leo was wriggling in his hands now, making it an effort to hold him up, but Kirk wasn't going to stop any time soon.

Each swipe of his tongue was a little lower, a little closer to the slick head of Leo's cock, and his mouth watered at the sight of it.

Leo shook and shivered, emitting delicious little moans, his hands clenched tight in Kirk's hair.

Kirk lowered his head, lifting Leo up a little higher at the same time, loving the feeling of controlling him like this. Leo's sweet, round little ass fit perfectly into his broad hands.

Then he took Leo into the slick heat of his mouth.

He didn't tease, didn't take it slow, with little licks and tormenting touches of his tongue; he might do that another time, he thought, when he had the patience for it.

He had little patience now, and the wolf had none at all.

Kirk sucked him in with almost brutal eagerness, pulling Leo forward so he could swallow more of his straining cock.

Leo moaned louder now, biting his lip, and said things like "Oh god," and "Oh *fuck*," as Kirk kept sucking him, pulling back only to thrust him forward again into that dark, wet heat.

He was using Leo, forcing him to fuck his face, and it felt *wonderful*.

Kirk set a tempo that was fast and merciless, swallowing around Leo's cock and sucking him with all the strength of his hot, hungry mouth. Oh, the sweet-salt taste of him, could he ever have enough of this?

"Oh god, stop, you're, I'm going to—" Leo babbled, pulling at Kirk's hair.

Kirk smiled a little, a smile that nobody could see.

He could feel it, that rising tide, in the flushed heat of Leo's skin and the pressure of his swelling cock inside Kirk's mouth.

Oh yes, he knew what Leo was saying, but he was hardly going to stop.

Let me drink you.

He sucked wetly, feeling his cheeks hollowing —and then, just as Leo threw back his head and groaned, Kirk shifted his grip on Leo's ass and pressed a fingertip into the cleft, barely grazing that tender hole.

Leo's breath stuttered. He ground out Kirk's name in a raw, uneven voice, his hands fisting in Kirk's hair, and came.

Ahh.

Kirk rode out the long pulses of salt—wet— heat, swallowing eagerly, breathing in the musky smell of Leo's come.

Mine, the wolf growled in his head, *mine.*

Leo shook as if he was coming apart, his skin damp with sweat, his breathing ragged and desperate.

One more long pulse, so wet and slick on his tongue, and then Leo was spent and softening.

Kirk still wouldn't allow him to slip free. He nuzzled and sucked, more gently now, pulling the very last drops from him until Leo nudged his shoulder: *stop.*

His jaw ached a little when he finally let Leo go. It was a good ache.

I need more practice, Kirk thought, with a giddy optimism that was entirely foreign and strange.

He'd been drunk on champagne once, and it had felt a little like this. The world was wider, brighter, and altogether better than an hour ago.

Licking his lips, Kirk lowered Leo down, stretching out his own long legs to set Leo on top of them.

Ahhh, yes, that was good. Leo's warm weight felt just right on top of him, and the sweetly muscled ridges of his stomach pressed against Kirk's own demanding arousal.

Leo's eyes were half-lidded, his expression dazed, but he was smiling.

"Mmm," he said softly, and wriggled a little, pressing closer against Kirk.

Low in his throat, Kirk growled. The feeling of Leo so tight and warm against him was making him lightheaded with need.

He slipped his arms around Leo's back, holding him close, holding him steady. *You are mine. You are safe.*

Leo sighed, a breathy little sound of happiness, then kissed the corner of his mouth, his brow, even the rough stubble of his cheek.

Kirk licked at the warm soft fold of his neck,

exploring the delicious scents trapped in the creases there, and Leo moaned sweetly into his ear.

"God, you—what you do to me," Leo said very softly, nuzzling at Kirk's ear and wriggling against him, rolling his hips in ways that were positively *wanton*.

Kirk couldn't take very much more of this.

He could feel the rising tide in himself now, the dizzying heat and need. The wolf was raging beneath it all, urging him to take his mate.

The wolf would not be denied.

Kirk spread his legs, letting Leo sink to the floor between them, and then surged forward.

Ah, the sweetness of it as Leo reacted to him instantly, giving in to the pressure of Kirk's chest and arms, letting himself be pushed down on his back on the wooden floor. His legs came up as he did so, shamelessly open and wide, folding around Kirk's hips.

Kirk paused for a moment to take in the sight of Leo like this, spread out before him like a feast: the rosy flush painting his fair skin from his neck to his upper chest, the small dent in his lush lower lip where his teeth grazed it, and the wide blue eyes with their dark pupils, so eager, so unafraid.

Maybe he should *be afraid*. He pushed that dark thought away. No. *Never.*

Leo rolled his head to the side, trying to see what Kirk was doing.

After bearing Leo to the floor, suddenly Kirk had stopped moving, stared at Leo, and moved away. It would be worrying if Leo wasn't feeling so blissed out, and if he couldn't hear Kirk rummaging through Leo's backpack no more than a couple of feet away, tossing out things that landed with soft thuds or rattles onto the old wooden floor.

Soon Kirk returned, carrying Leo's folded-up sleeping bag and some small white shape that Leo couldn't make out in the dim light.

With one swift motion, Kirk lifted Leo's lower body up and put the folded sleeping bag under him.

Oh. Leo could feel himself blushing, a swift rush of heat.

Lying here like this felt very exposed. The thick soft sleeping bag pushed up his ass, making it natural to tilt his hips and let his legs fall open wide to either side.

It felt *wicked.*

He had to crane his neck to see what Kirk was doing. He was tilting the white thing over his open hand, upending it—*oh.*

Leo recognized the shape now. It was a small bottle of hand lotion that he'd stowed away in his pack..

The sight of that white dollop of lotion in Kirk's hand sent a jolt straight to Leo's cock, spent though it was.

He couldn't take his eyes off Kirk: even as he crouched there, he still looked just as huge and dangerous as his animal self, with his wild mane of dark hair spilling over his shoulders, and his massive arms bunching as he shook the bottle and let more white lotion drip into his hand.

So much larger than Leo, so much stronger.

So much of him, and all mine.

Then Kirk slipped a slippery hand between his splayed-open legs, and Leo couldn't help moaning.

Kirk's hands were as big as the rest of him, big

and warm and strong, and they were pinning him down, opening him up. Kirk's left hand pushed carefully at his wounded leg, positioning him so he could slip his leg around Kirk's back, safe and out of the way.

And Kirk's other hand was right *there*, spreading lotion between his cheeks, pushing insistently into his cleft.

Kirk's eyes were dark, feral almost, and he looked so hungry. His gaze devoured Leo, cataloguing every inch of him, every tiny hitch in his breathing, every tremble in his legs as they were bent back even farther.

Leo felt bare and vulnerable like this, with his legs spread and bent, his hips tilted up, and Kirk looming over him. Bare and vulnerable and incredibly turned on.

"God, yes, please, do it," Leo babbled, barely aware of what he was saying. "Do it, do it, *fuck*—"

He was begging now, so desperately turned on he could barely breathe, and that was only with the tip of Kirk's finger inside him.

That thick finger moved deeper now, slick and wet and warm, testing him.

Leo gasped, feeling the flush of warm blood in his face as Kirk watched him intently, his finger delving deeper with every tiny thrust.

He could feel himself clinging to every callus of Kirk's finger, and his breath stuttered when Kirk smiled. Oh, just a tiny smile, a crooked tilt in the strong lines of his mouth—but for him, it was a lot.

"So tight," Kirk breathed, in that low dark voice that was pure sex.

Leo felt himself heat up to the very tips of his ears.

He squirmed, pushing forward a little against Kirk, trying to urge him on.

Yes, he *was* tight, he hadn't done this for a long time, and even that one finger felt like a stretch, given how huge Kirk's hands were.

But he wasn't going to stop *now.*

Kirk felt like a starving beggar invited to a banquet. He had Leo spread out before him like a feast, and fingering him open took almost more patience than he was capable of.

Almost.

It took slow, careful strokes of his fingers—two now—and with each stroke, Leo moaned, a little sound that he tried to muffle by biting his lower lip.

Kirk felt himself straining to keep control; he was harder than he'd ever been before.

"Oh god," Leo said huskily, "just—do it, don't —tease—" His breathing stuttered as he tried to lift up his head, trying to see Kirk's fingers fucking him.

Kirk crooked his fingers a little inside Leo, searching, and watched with a rush of intense satisfaction as Leo's features crumpled with pleasure.

He'd found the right spot.

"Ohh," Leo moaned, his face flushing again. His skin was so fair, and Kirk found his blushes irresistible.

Slowly, Leo relaxed around his fingers, and that tight muscle began to open.

Kirk added more lotion, then slicked up his own cock with as light a touch as he could manage.

It was difficult not to give in to the urge to grip himself in a tight fist and jack hard and fast—jack himself off in front of Leo's eyes, come all over his stomach—but he wanted so much more than that.

Leo licked his lips, bright spots of color burning on his cheeks, as Kirk lined himself up with Leo.

The sight of that pink tongue-tip against the darker red of Leo's lips made Kirk shiver hotly.

Oh, that lush mouth, how he wanted it wrapped around his cock. How he wanted to feel what it was like to push himself down that hot, wet mouth, holding Leo by the hair. He could almost imagine it, but he knew the reality would be better.

Focus.

In the back of his mind, he could feel the wolf becoming impatient with him, growling at him. Wolves didn't really understand past or future or anything that involved forecasting what might happen: for wolves, there was only the now.

This *now*.

The *now* where Kirk's cockhead was right against Leo's tight entrance, and he was beginning to push in.

"Ohh," Leo moaned. His stomach muscles tensed visibly.

God, the tightness of him!

Kirk cursed under his breath, feeling the hot burn of resistance as he slowly drove himself forward.

Leo's scent changed just a fraction, gaining a smoky note that Kirk couldn't quite place.

Kirk paused, lifted his head, and watched the frown lines on Leo's face smooth out.

"Sorry, god, you're so—I haven't done this in —" Leo said, biting his lip as if to prevent the words from spilling out. "Don't stop, just…"

"Slow?" Kirk said. It was an effort still,

producing words from a throat that wanted only to growl and snarl and howl.

"Yeah," Leo said, with a small smile that did unspeakable things to Kirk's self-control.

Slow. Right.

He held himself back, his arms shaking with the effort of it, just as Leo's tight muscles were resisting him, clenching down on him as if to try and push him back out.

Clamping down on the demands of his body, Kirk waited. He was still barely inside.

Leo breathed carefully, slowly, and the frown lines didn't return to his face. That was good.

The tension seemed to ratchet down a little, and as Leo's breaths grew less fractured, Kirk began to feel Leo's body yielding to him.

That surrender was so sweet that it stole his breath. Leo's resistance was giving way, slowly but surely.

Every tiny movement of Leo's body felt like an invitation to go faster, to just *take* him. Every hitching breath made Kirk's own breath come faster, until they were breathing in a fast, syncopated rhythm.

And still he went slow, so slow, giving Leo time to get used to him.

It wasn't easy.

Inside, the wolf was *snarling*, and Kirk could feel sweat beginning to gather at the nape of his neck, under the heavy weight of his hair.

He would not break. He would not let the wolf slip free to hurt Leo.

Leo moaned softly, then gave an experimental push of his hips that made Kirk see stars.

"Okay," Leo breathed, then smiled again as if whatever he could see in Kirk's face pleased him. "That feels—yeah."

Kirk took a deep, shuddering breath; his hands were trembling.

Then he began to drive himself into Leo, inch by inch. Slow, still so slow, but relentless.

"Oh god, oh—don't stop—damn," Leo gasped. His hands curled into loose fists, and he thumped the wooden floor as if to mark the rhythm of Kirk's progress.

Kirk blinked away the sweat that was gathering on his forehead. Leo was still so tight around him, hot and tight and clinging, and the sensation of breaching him like this was incredible. It felt like he was breaking Leo and re-forming him, fitting him like a glove around the heft of his cock.

Leo closed his eyes and rolled his head to the side when Kirk was still no more than halfway in, breathing fast.

Watching him, seeing the tight lines at the corners of his eyes, Kirk checked himself with an immense effort, but Leo whispered harshly, "Keep— *going.*"

He did.

He kept going, even though he could feel the pressure, the resistance.

Leo made little breathy sounds as he fucked him open, sounds that Kirk would pay good money to record and play back later.

Closer now, closer still. He shifted, pulling Leo's lower body up against him for easier access.

That changed the angle of his thrusts, driving them directly over that sensitive spot, stimulating it mercilessly.

In response, Leo began to moan, making more noise than before, as if he was no longer worried about being heard. Not that anyone would, except perhaps the bats; but Kirk had the feeling that Leo wasn't used to that much privacy.

"Good," Kirk said, as softly as he could, and pushed *in*.

Leo moaned at a higher pitch. He rolled his hips in a tight little half-circle as his body finally yielded to the relentless pressure.

Kirk could feel himself sliding deeper, closer, and he took a deep breath and gave the last push to sheathe himself completely.

Now he was in Leo to the hilt, his hips all the way against Leo's thighs.

It felt amazing. It felt *right.*

He waited for a moment, pacing himself, feasting his eyes on the sight of Leo spread open for him. He couldn't look away from the sight of his own cock disappearing into Leo's rosy-pink flesh. He was spreading Leo's lovely round ass wide open, filling him up so tightly that it didn't even seem possible for the whole length of his hard shaft to fit inside him.

Leo's breaths came even faster now, and he moaned continuously; small broken noises that only increased when Kirk began to move.

"God—you're so big," Leo whispered. "Yes—oh god—like that—"

Kirk withdrew slowly, then thrust into him hard and fast, loving the slick yield of his body even as Leo gasped out a curse.

He was no longer trying to be careful. Careful was a long way behind, now.

All that mattered now was *this:* the fiery connection between them, the harsh loud sound of their joined breathing, and Leo's fists thumping erratically on the floor.

Ahh, the heat of him, the clinging, demanding clench of him!

Kirk heard the wolf growling, and he was no longer sure if it was only in the back of his mind.

Sweat dripped down from stray curls of his hair, and he snapped his hips hard against Leo's thighs, pounding him open.

Mine. Mine. *Mine.*

Leo was lifting himself up even higher, using his good leg to give himself leverage, pushing himself up to be used.

Kirk took him.

The sounds they were making seemed so loud that they could be heard for miles around: a clarion call and a warning.

There was nothing but this, nothing but the slick wet heat and friction, the dim light illuminating Leo's screwed-up face and half-open, gasping mouth, and the sounds of their bodies slapping together with lewd, wet sounds.

Leo groaned, a desperate sound, and one of his hands came up to tug at his own cock. It was rising again, still a little short of full mast, but with every thrust it grew harder, and the jerky movements of his fist grew faster.

Kirk sniffed, taking in the lush scent of Leo's arousal, stronger and richer now. It went to his head like wine, and he felt almost dizzy with lust.

He slowed down, then pulled himself all the way out, smiling a little as Leo protested, "No, what—

don't stop *now*—no—"

"Shh," Kirk said, and then he took a deep
breath and forced himself back in.

Leo was so tight and warm and ready for him
that Kirk drove into him to the hilt, in one long sliding
brutal thrust.

As Kirk slid himself home, Leo *wailed.* His
other hand came up to pound on Kirk's shoulder, even
as his hips jerked up and Leo came all over his own
fingers.

The shudders of Leo's body as he came were
delicious. Kirk felt every one of them on his cock, little
tremors that pulled at him like fingers, and the scent of
his seed made Kirk's mouth water.

Groaning, Kirk slammed into Leo, angling his
hips to push even deeper. He tried to shake back his
sweat-damp hair, but it fell forward again as he
withdrew. Then he thrust again, deep and hard and
relentless.

Leo made harsh, broken sounds that weren't
words, only noise, and Kirk heard himself groaning, a
low continuous drone of sound.

Pleasure sang along his spine with every thrust,

and he knew he couldn't hold out much longer.

Leo's hand was still cupped around his cock, and his stomach was wet with his own seed. It was an irresistible sight; Kirk wanted to lunge forward and lick it off him.

He couldn't bend himself in half like that, but he could do—this.

His back bowed with the force of his thrust, and he felt Leo clenching down on him deliberately, his flesh constricting on the hard length inside him.

"Do it—" Leo told him, his voice shaky and raw. "Do it, come in me, fuck me—"

That was all it took. With one last, brutal thrust, Kirk fell over the edge.

Kirk held on to the curve of Leo's hips with both hands as his body shook itself apart.

It felt like it wouldn't stop, like these pulses of white-hot pleasure would just keep coming and coming and—coming, oh fuck…

He growled again, and this time it definitely wasn't just in the back of his mind. A possessive haze blurred out his vision, and he knew he was gripping

Leo too tightly as he spilled his seed inside, but he couldn't stop.

Take it, take my seed, you're *mine*.

His head was swimming with the scent and feel of Leo's body against him, so sweet and warm and open now, so ready for him. He wished he could keep going, keep fucking him for hours until they were both exhausted and covered in come.

Kirk threw back his head and howled as the last long delicious pulse forced itself out of him.

Feeling limp and weak with the power of that release, he withdrew himself from Leo as slowly as he could, and then he fell forward, like a tree toppling.

His landing was soft.

Leo felt as though he'd been run over by a steam train.

He huffed a breath, trying to find his voice again. His throat was as scratchy as though he'd been yelling his lungs out. Maybe he had.

He pushed at Kirk's head, which rested like a heavy, warm weight on top of his chest, trying to rouse him.

Kirk grunted something indecipherable. It sounded like a complaint.

The weight of him pinned Leo down on the rucked-up sleeping bag, and his leg was beginning to cramp.

Leo bucked up with a tremendous twist of his hips, and even that didn't dislodge Kirk, but it shook him into something approaching wakefulness.

Kirk rolled up on one elbow, dark hair hanging in his eyes. "Mmmm," he said, on a faintly interrogative note.

Leo had to smile, even as he pushed at Kirk's massive shoulders, trying to get him to take more of his weight off Leo's stomach.

"Mmm to you too," he said, his voice husky and soft with a tenderness he couldn't hide. "That was amazing. You—you are..." His voice trailed off, and he knew he was blushing again.

Crap. Smooth moves, Leo.

Kirk shook his long hair back, which didn't help at all as it fell forward again immediately, and then he trailed a big warm hand along Leo's jaw, tilting his face up.

Leo closed his eyes, hoping to be kissed. Then he felt Kirk's arms slide around his shoulders, lifting him until they were both sitting up, leaning against each other like bookends.

"Aahh," he sighed happily as he was positioned against Kirk's chest. He felt warm and safe and completely exhausted, but that was all right.

Everything was all right, now.

Kirk's mouth came down on his, then roved

over his ear, his neck. Kisses that were rough and passionate and possessive, like brands.

Leo moaned a little and tipped his head back against Kirk's shoulder, offering him his throat.

He didn't know why he needed to do that, but he knew it was the right thing to do; he felt it in every bone of his body.

And he felt Kirk's reaction: the way he sucked in his breath, all his muscles suddenly tensing into rock hardness, then slowly easing again with a long sigh that spoke of utter satisfaction.

Kirk kissed his throat, licking gently at his adam's apple, a strange and ticklish sensation that had Leo wriggling in his arms, then took his mouth again and again.

Leo leaned back in his strong arms and offered himself up for more hot, wet, demanding kisses that melted his bones to jelly.

He slipped a hand beneath the heavy, sweat-damp weight of Kirk's hair, enjoying the way the curly strands clung to his fingers, then sprang up again.

Kirk's teeth closed gently over his jaw, then nibbled at his ear.

Hot breath washed over his ear, and Leo giggled foolishly, squirming in Kirk's arms. His limp, spent cock gave a little half-hearted twitch.

"Oh god, don't start me up again, I can't take anymore," Leo said, laughing. "You wrung me out like a rag, you beast."

Kirk was suddenly very still, his muscles tensing up again.

With a wince, Leo realized what he'd said. "No, I didn't mean—" he began, then stopped when the easy flow of words dried up. He had no idea how to fix this. If it *could* be fixed.

"It's true," Kirk said then, a deep rumble of sound that vibrated through Leo's chest. "I am." He paused, and Leo could *feel* the effort it cost him when Kirk finally added, "A beast."

It sounded like a condemnation. *This is what I am. This is all I am.*

Leo didn't believe that for a minute.

He shook his head, then deliberately reached up and pulled at Kirk's hair, drawing him closer for another kiss.

Kirk resisted him, but it only lasted for a heartbeat, and then the tension between them slowly melted away into another delicious, burning kiss.

When Kirk's lips finally, reluctantly slid away, Leo took a breath.

"I don't care," he said.

Kirk's dark eyes bored into his, as if he was trying to convince himself Leo wasn't lying.

Leo looked back at him, meeting that probing gaze head-on.

Then he nuzzled at Kirk's jaw.

"You're still you," he said.

Kirk couldn't believe his good fortune. Really, truly couldn't believe it. He wasn't sure it was real.

What did I do to deserve this, he asked himself, shivering when Leo began to nip leisurely at his jaw, little sharp-toothed bites. He had teeth like a fox, small and white and pointy.

Kirk's body still echoed with the delicious lassitude that came after sex. He felt utterly relaxed and sated, and even the wolf was at peace, curled up and asleep inside his mind.

Leo smiled up at him, a warm weight in his arms, and Kirk bent his head and kissed him again, unable to resist that golden smile. It was imperative to claim Leo's mouth again and again, until he grew lightheaded enough to pause for breath.

Leo stroked his shoulder, and a small tension gathered in him that Kirk could interpret with reasonable confidence; he knew Leo was going to ask him something before he spoke.

"So, this…transformation," Leo began, "It's—going to happen again?"

Kirk nodded. It was an effort not to look away.

He'd never shared his secret with anyone, not after the others on his team were dead. He'd never thought he would ever *want* to share his secret with anyone.

"Tonight," he told Leo, wincing as Leo's eyes widened. "And the night after."

Leo shook his head as if to clear it. "But—not every night, right?"

"Only around full moon," Kirk said, surprised. Somehow he'd thought that was self-evident. He shrugged, and made a desperate attempt to treat the subject lightly. "You know. Like in the movies. Werewolf."

"Oh," Leo said, and then he began to hiccup with laughter.

Kirk stared at him, surprised beyond words. Of all the reactions he might have considered, this wasn't one of them.

He took Leo's shoulders in his hands and shook him gently. "Leo?"

"Sorry," Leo said, his eyes still creased with laughter. "It's just—well, you didn't give me a whole lot of time to *think*, did you? I'm sure I would have figured it out on my own, only—" He laughed again, a little burst of merriment. "I thought you—the other you—I thought you were a *dog*."

Kirk's eyebrows rose. "A dog," he said, deadpan.

"You were wearing a collar!" Leo protested, sputtering with laughter.

Then his whole face changed and the laugh lines disappeared. He stared at Kirk's neck, undamaged under the patches of dried blood. "You were *bleeding*. It looked painful. What—"

"I heal," Kirk told him. "Fast."

"Wow," Leo said, still staring. "No kidding." He pressed a kiss into Kirk's shoulder, soft and warm and tender. "I'm glad you're okay."

Kirk nodded.

It was easier, now, to speak of it. Leo's laughter

had broken the tension, and in this moment, the shame in which he'd always cloaked his secret seemed to disappear like mist before the morning sun. It was just a fact. He was a werewolf, and he could heal fast. One day, he might even be able to tell Leo how it had happened.

Gratefully, Kirk wrapped his arms tighter around Leo.

"You?" he asked. "Your leg?"

He knew, thanks to scent and touch, that Leo was hurting, but that it wasn't too bad, that his leg was healing as well as it could. But he wanted to hear it from his mouth.

Leo's courage still astonished him. Leo had gone out into the dark woods alone to find Kirk, walking on a bad leg and carrying vivid, painful memories of that old bear trap clawing him open. For all Leo knew, there could be traps everywhere in these woods. But he'd still gone, with only an old map to show him the way. The map Kirk's father had marked with an X.

"Not too bad," Leo said with a small shrug. "Not going to run any marathons this morning, that's for sure."

Kirk smiled and kissed the top of his head. "Understood."

They rested against each other for a while, warm and content, and Kirk sent his senses out to scout the ridge and the forest beyond.

The birdsong was bright and chatty this morning, and there was a black bear snuffling around a berry bush some distance away. Rain on the wind, and the scent of woodsmoke from some forester's fire a mile away.

And further afield, near his cabin...

He stiffened abruptly, anger washing over him in a cold wave.

Leo blinked. "Kirk? What's wrong?"

Miles away, Kirk could hear the sound of motorcycles. At least twenty motorcycles, coming up the dirt road that led to his cabin.

He remembered that scent he'd smelled before in town, the utter wrongness of it, the way it made his hackles rise.

The drone of the motorcyles never changed, and it was steadily coming closer.

The riders weren't going for a scenic drive.

They ignored all the side roads that led away from the cabin and crept up the mountainside bend by hairpin bend, closer and closer.

They were trespassing on his territory.

They were coming for *him*.

ABOUT THE AUTHOR

Isabel Dare has always loved sexy, steamy and perversely romantic tales, from 'The Story of O' to 'The Persian Boy'.

Isabel is presently hard at work on the sequel to this book, *Wolf Howl*.

If you want to know when it's available, please sign up for Isabel Dare's new release e-mail list at isabeldare.com!

Printed in Great Britain
by Amazon.co.uk, Ltd.,
Marston Gate.